R[illegible]FT'S LAST CASE

A captivating Victorian historical murder mystery

KERRY TOMBS

Inspector Ravenscroft Detective Mysteries Book 10

JOFFE BOOKS

First published 2020
Joffe Books, London
www.joffebooks.com

ISBN 978-1-78931-562-2

PROLOGUE

APRIL 1836

The wind drove the rain into his face. A small boy, clutching his posy of flowers, slowly followed his parents up the winding path towards the churchyard at the top of the hill.

'Come now,' said his father, opening the creaking gate. 'There is duty to be done.'

The family made their way between the rows of neat headstones, his mother pausing for a moment and then reaching out for the boy's hand as he caught up with his parents.

This journey was familiar. Perhaps they had brought him here last year?

Then they reached the grave, and stood in silence for a while, the boy straining to read the letters cut deep into the stone.

'Anne would have been seven today, had she lived,' said his mother, bending down and placing a small bunch of flowers on the grave.

'It was not to be, Kitty. The Lord took her away from us, and she is with him now, and at peace,' said his father in a solemn voice.

The boy looked down nervously at the ground.

'Remember your sister now.' His mother squeezed his hand.

The boy reached out and laid his tribute of flowers up against the cold stone.

'Let us now pray,' said his father.

The boy closed his eyes tightly. If he tried hard enough, he might be able to conjure up a picture of this sister. She had died before he had been born, and yet she had always been a part of his life.

'Amen,' concluded his father.

'Mama, tell me about Anne?' the boy asked his mother, a question he had asked many times before.

'Why, she was the sweetest, loveliest infant that you have ever seen, and we loved her dearly.'

'Would she have liked me?'

'Now, why ever do you ask that for?'

'Would she have liked me?' the boy repeated his question, looking up intently into his mother's saddened face.

'Of course she would. Anne loved everyone, and we loved her, that is why we come here every year, to remember her and to pray.'

'Will you pray for me when I am gone?'

'Good Lord, child!' exclaimed his father. 'Don't talk such nonsense. We will die long before you.'

'No, no, I don't want you to die,' cried out the boy, tears welling up in his eyes.

'Everyone has to die, son, but we don't intend dying for a long while yet, if the good Lord allows. You have no need to fret on that account.'

'I don't want you to die.'

His mother reached out for him and drew him close. 'There now, don't worry, my boy. Don't upset yourself so foolishly. Dry your tears. Anne would not want to see you crying. You must do something for me.'

'Anything you say, Mama.'

‘You must promise me that you will never forget your sister. You must always remember that Anne was your sister. Will you do that for me and your father?’

‘Yes, yes,’ said the boy desperately, clinging to his mother.

‘Good boy. Now then, dry your eyes. I know that you will always be a good son to us. I am sure that when you grow up you will go on to do many great things in your life. You will grow into a fine young man one day. You will make your father and me proud that you are our son. Perhaps when you are older you will marry and have children of your own. But always remember, son, no matter what you achieve in this life, that Anne was your sister. She will always be with us. She will never leave any of us. You see that, don’t you?’

‘Yes.’

‘Anne will always watch over you, Samuel. She will keep you safe from all adversity. She will be your guiding light. Remember — Anne Ravenscroft.’

CHAPTER ONE

WORCESTER, THURSDAY, 13 APRIL 1893

Ravenscroft hesitated as he approached the door. For two years he had feared that this day would finally arrive. Now he was about to face the inevitable, and the prospect was not to his liking.

He had asked himself a number of times over the previous few months, whether or not there would be some way in which the decision might be delayed, but he knew in his heart that time had finally caught up with him. There were no other options available to him.

After removing his spectacles and cleaning them on his handkerchief, and then mopping his balding head, he took a deep breath and tapped at the door gently.

'Come in!' said a voice from within.

Ravenscroft pushed open the door.

'Detective Inspector Ravenscroft, is it not?' said a distinguished-looking gentleman, glancing up from his chair behind the large desk.

'Yes, Chief Constable.'

'Take a chair, man.'

'Thank you, sir.'

'I don't believe we have met before, Ravenscroft?'

'No, sir.'

'I've only been here for about two months, you know.'

'So I believe, sir.'

'I thought it was about time that I caught up with a few things.'

'Yes, sir,' replied Ravenscroft dutifully.

'Not let me see, where is your history?' His superior reached out towards a number of files on his desk, before selecting one and opening it. 'It says here that you joined us from Whitechapel in London, in 1888?'

'That is correct.'

'That was the year those Ripper murders took place there wasn't it?'

'Yes, sir.'

'You didn't have much luck in catching the fellow.'

'I left some months before the outrages took place,' replied Ravenscroft, detecting a slight scathing tone in his superior's voice.

'Just as well, I suppose. Married with two young children, I see.'

'I married late in life.'

'Good health?'

'I have slight asthma. Nothing that prevents me from carrying out my duties.'

'So you have been with us for nearly five years now?'

'That is correct.'

'I see that during your time here your record has been quite good. You appear to have been successful in bringing quite a few villains to justice. I would not have thought there was that much crime going on in such a small country town as Ledbury.'

'You are correct in that assumption, sir. Several of my cases have involved travelling around the Three Counties.'

'So I see. It states here that you even went to New York.' The Chief Constable stared hard at the detective over his pince-nez.

'I covered the costs of the journey, sir.'

'Yes, well, it all looks very good, I must say. A good record, indeed, something to be proud about.'

'Thank you, sir.'

'However I have noticed one thing, of which I am sure you are aware.'

'Oh, what would that be, sir?' replied Ravenscroft forcing a brief smile.

'Your age, man. According to my calculations you should have retired two years ago.'

'Really, sir,' replied Ravenscroft trying to look surprised.

'Come now, let us not shilly-shally about. I am sure you are more than fully aware of that fact,' retorted the Chief Constable. 'I don't know how my predecessor overlooked such an error. I expect you will be looking forward to putting your feet up now.'

'Not really, sir. I enjoy the work.'

'Plenty of time to do the gardening, take the wife and children away. You look quite a fit man, Ravenscroft. I'm sure there may be plenty of other opportunities for you.'

'I can't think of any at present,' said a downcast Ravenscroft.

'You will in time. Now we shall have to find a replacement for you. I understand that your junior is a Sergeant Cribb?'

'Sergeant Crabb, sir,' corrected Ravenscroft.

'I believe he was only recently promoted to Sergeant, and anyway he is far too young. No, we will have to cast our net wider. I don't suppose you have anyone in mind?' The Chief Constable stroked his large moustache.

'I have never given the matter that much thought. I am quite prepared to stay on for a year or more, if it would help.'

'No, no, that is quite out of the question. You must go, and that is an end to the matter.' His superior abruptly closed the file and threw it down on to the desk.

Ravenscroft sighed. 'And when might that be?'

'By rights, it should be today, but look here Ravenscroft, you are a good man and you have done noble work for us. I can see that you are dedicated to your job. God knows, we could do with more men like you.'

'Might I suggest that I might leave at the end of the year? That would give you plenty of time to find a replacement, and for me to work with him, show him around, as it were,' suggested Ravenscroft, realising that he was clutching at straws.

'No, no, we cannot have that. Another nine months would be quite unethical. Let's say — to the end of the month?'

'With all due respect, sir, that is only two and a half weeks away. Perhaps three months might be better, to allow for a more orderly transition?'

'Out of the question! I will allow you to the end of the month, and that is my final word. There is nothing more to say.'

'I see,' said Ravenscroft with reluctance.

'Cheer up! This time next year you will be a new man and wonder why you did not leave sooner.'

'I doubt that, sir.'

'Now, just before you go, Ravenscroft, what do you know about spiritualism?'

'Very little. I don't hold with such nonsense.'

'Oh, why do you say that?'

'I don't believe that it is possible to communicate with the dead. I do know, however, that there are unsavoury people who would take advantage of the bereaved.'

'I am inclined to agree with you. Take a look at this.' The Chief Constable passed over an envelope to Ravenscroft. 'It came in the post this morning.'

Ravenscroft took the envelope, removed the letter and read its contents.

'What do you think?'

'It was written three days ago. If you want my honest opinion, I would say that the writer is of disturbed mind.'

'Read it again, out loud, if you will.'

'My dear sir,

You must help me. On Sunday evening we had our séance as usual, and Old Crabbit says my time is shortly up, and that it will all be over with me by the weekend. As I don't want to die, you must help me. Please send your best officer.

Your most obedient servant,
Miss Maud Fincher.
Claremont,
Colwall.'

'Well?'

'The writer has clearly had an upsetting experience at this séance and believes that someone from the spirit world is seeking some kind of revenge on her,' answered Ravenscroft. 'I have encountered one or two of these so-called mediums in the past and have found them to be nothing more than charlatans and quacks preying on vulnerable people.'

'I see.'

'Unfortunately we cannot arrest these people for being members of a spiritualist organisation.'

'Quite. So what do you think we should do with this letter?'

'Ignore it,' suggested Ravenscroft. 'The woman clearly has an over-excitable imagination. We will probably hear nothing else from her. However, I see from the envelope that the letter was addressed to you, and possibly sent to your home address.'

'I thought it would not be long before you noticed that.'

'The lady is known personally to you?'

'To my wife. They are both on the local Worcestershire Committee for raising funds for Doctor Barnardo's children's homes.'

'It is a worthwhile undertaking.'

'I have never met Miss Fincher in person, and I believe that she has only a passing acquaintance with my wife, who must have mentioned my position.' The Chief Constable shuffled his papers around on his desk for some seconds before speaking. 'This places me, and the force, in a difficult position, as I am sure you will appreciate. It does seem as though someone, whether they be dead or alive, is threatening Miss Fincher. It would never do if something happened to this woman, and we were seen not to have done anything about it. I hope I am making myself clear. It would reflect very badly on us. I think you should look into it, Ravenscroft. Go and see this woman, put her mind at rest and all that.'

'Why not send the local constable to pay her a visit?'

'No, no, that won't do at all. It should be someone senior and experienced. I am confident that you are the right man for the job.'

'If you insist, sir,' said Ravenscroft rising from his seat.

'Good man. Keep the letter. Take it with you. Good day Ravenscroft — oh, and keep me informed of any developments.'

'Of course, sir,' replied the detective, taking his leave.

* * *

'So there you have it, Tom. I must retire at the end of the month, and that is that,' said Ravenscroft later that afternoon, as the police trap made its way round the winding road, down from the Wyche Cutting on the westerly slopes of the Malvern Hills.

'It does not seem right to me, sir,' said Sergeant Crabb.

'I know, but there is nothing I can do about it. You will have to get used to working with someone else, I am afraid.'

'I don't fancy that. I think I shall resign my position and probably go back to the family farm.'

'You cannot do that, Tom. You have a wife and three young children to support. You are young and still have a promising career in front of you. The force needs you. You must stay.'

'I don't know. It will not be the same without you,' said Crabb reluctantly.

'Anyway, enough of that for now. What did you make of that letter?'

'The lady certainly seems to be frightened by something, or someone.'

'The trouble is, some of these women have very little to occupy their minds, living in country houses with nothing to do all day, they often let their imagination play tricks on them.'

'It seems that way.'

'If it wasn't for the fact that this Miss Fincher is an acquaintance of the Chief Constable's wife, we would not be concerning ourselves with this nonsense at all, but I'm afraid we have little choice in the matter. All we can do is hear the woman out, and try to allay her fears, and then we can go back to Ledbury and do some proper policing.'

As the trap began its descent into Colwall village, they observed a postman walking along the side of the road.

'We are looking for Claremont. I would be obliged if you could assist us,' called out Ravenscroft.

'Claremont is the next house down on the left, sir,' replied the postman, touching his cap.

'Thank you, my man,' said Ravenscroft, as Crabb urged the horse on. 'That must be it there,' called out Ravenscroft, leaning forwards to look at an old Georgian building at the side of the road.

Crabb brought the horse to a standstill. 'It looks as though it has seen better days.'

'I am inclined to agree with you. Overgrown ivy and flaking paintwork suggest a certain degree of neglect on the part of its owner,' remarked Ravenscroft as he stepped down from the trap.

Crabb secured the horse and made sure it was watered, then the two men walked up the short drive towards the house.

Ravenscroft pulled hard on the rusty bell-pull, and after a short interval the door was opened by a middle-aged woman with slightly greying hair and worn features, dressed in maid's attire.

'Good afternoon. My name is Detective Inspector Ravenscroft, and this is my colleague Detective Sergeant Crabb, from the police station in Ledbury. We would be obliged if you would inform your mistress of our arrival.'

'I am sorry, sir. I am afraid I cannot do that,' replied the maid, in a hesitant tone of voice.

Ravenscroft was perplexed. 'This is Claremont, is it not?'

'Yes, sir.'

'Then I assume it is the residence of Miss Maud Fincher?'

'Yes, sir.'

'I believe that your mistress would be prepared to see us. If you would kindly inform her of our arrival, I would be obliged.'

'You cannot see Miss Fincher. It is not possible,' replied the maid.

'Look here—'

'You cannot see Miss Fincher.'

'But why ever not?'

'Because my mistress is dead!'

CHAPTER TWO

'Dead!' exclaimed Ravenscroft.

'My mistress died two days ago.'

Ravenscroft was somewhat taken aback by the news. 'How did Miss Fincher die?'

'I last saw her on Monday evening when she retired for the night. When I knocked on her door on Tuesday morning there was no reply, so I entered the bedroom and found her dead,' said the maid, looking sorrowfully down at the floor.

'We are sorry for your loss. I wonder if we might come inside?' asked Ravenscroft.

'I don't understand, sir. May I enquire why you are here? Neither the doctor nor I have sent for the police.'

'Your mistress wrote us a letter on Monday, saying that she was in fear of her life. Unfortunately I was not personally in receipt of the letter until this morning, otherwise we would have come earlier.'

The maid stared hard at the two detectives for some moments before speaking. 'I think you had better enter, sir.'

'Thank you.' Ravenscroft removed his hat as he and Crabb stepped into a dimly lit hall. 'You say you found your mistress dead on Tuesday morning? May I enquire as to what was the cause of her demise?'

'She had a weak heart. She had been complaining of it for some months.'

'I see. So you found Miss Fincher dead in her bed?'

'Oh no, she was lying on the floor by the side of the bed. She must have been trying to get up in the night when her heart gave way, and she fell to the floor. There was nothing I could do for her. She was quite cold.' The maid began to cry.

'I am sorry to cause any distress. I appreciate how difficult this is for you. What did you do when you found your mistress?'

'I closed up the house and went into the village to summon Doctor Cranbrook. He came straight away and confirmed that Miss Fincher was . . .' Her voice trailed away.

'And where is your mistress now?'

'She is at the undertaker's in Malvern Link.'

'Might we see the bedroom where your mistress died?' asked Ravenscroft.

'I don't understand why you would want to do that,' said the maid.

'It is just procedure. When someone dies like this, unexpectedly, we have to see where the death took place,' answered Ravenscroft uneasily.

The maid dabbed her eyes, before leading the way up an old creaking staircase, and along a short corridor. 'This is Miss Fincher's room.'

'Thank you — and your room is where?'

'It is on the next floor, in the attic.'

'Would you have heard your mistress call out in the night, if she had done so?' asked Ravenscroft.

'I doubt it, sir. My room is situated at the back of the house.'

'Are there any other servants here?' enquired Crabb.

'No, I am the only one. I do the cooking and cleaning, as well as looking after my mistress.'

'You have been with Miss Fincher for some time?' asked Ravenscroft.

'I have been here for seven months.'

'Oh? What happened to the previous maid?'

'I believe she left to get married.'

'Might we see inside the room?' Ravenscroft gave an encouraging smile.

The maid opened the door, and the two detectives stepped into a well-furnished but dimly lit bedroom, where a strong smell of mothballs and carbolic soap hung in the air.

'Has anything been touched in here since Miss Fincher died, or any windows opened?' asked Ravenscroft, looking at the large bed in the centre of the room.

'I did close the window after I found my mistress, but I could not bring myself to clean in here,' said the maid in scarcely more than a whisper.

'I quite understand. Can you show us where you found the body?'

The maid pointed to a bedside rug, situated to one side of the bed.

'I see — the sheets show where Miss Fincher left her bed. Was she lying on her back, or her front, when you found her?

'On her front. She must have been trying to make her way to the bell-pull.'

'Yes, I see that it is on the wall over there, by the side of the fireplace. That is connected to your bedroom, so that if Miss Fincher wanted anything in the night she could summon you?'

'Yes, sir.'

Ravenscroft walked over to the large sash window and looked through the glass down at the driveway below. 'But she did not call you on the night in question?'

'No, sir.'

'It looks as though she was trying to make her way to the bell-pull when she collapsed. Tell me . . . er.'

'My name is Gladys Brotherton.'

'Tell me, Gladys, did your mistress take any medication?'

'Yes, all her medicines are on the bedside cabinet over there.'

Ravenscroft picked up the coloured bottles, studying the labels upon them, before unscrewing the caps and smelling their contents.

'Pardon me, sir, but when you arrived you said mistress had written you a letter saying she was in fear of her life?'

'Yes. I have the letter here. Would you look at it, please?' Ravenscroft removed the letter from his inside pocket and passed it over to the maid. 'Can you confirm that is Miss Fincher's handwriting?'

'It is, sir. I remember posting the letter on Monday afternoon. I was not aware of its contents, of course.'

'In the letter she mentions someone called "Old Crabbit" — can you tell us anything about this person?'

'I have not heard the name before.' Gladys handed the letter back to Ravenscroft.

'Did your mistress have any enemies?'

'Why, no.'

'There is no one that would have cause to do her harm?' persisted Ravenscroft.

'Miss Fincher was the kindest, most gentle person ever to be placed upon this earth. She never did any harm to anyone. I don't understand all this,' replied the maid, looking concerned.

'That is good to know. Your mistress mentions a séance of some kind — can you tell us anything about that?'

'Yes, she did attend such events.'

'How often did these séances happen?'

'Once a week, on a Sunday afternoon.'

'Were they usually held here?' asked Ravenscroft, intrigued.

'Sometimes here. On other occasions, they took place at the homes of the other members of the group.'

'Did you attend these séances?'

'No. I do not hold with that kind of thing,' replied the maid with a look of disapproval.

'So there was a regular group of people who attended these séances? How many people were there?'

'Usually five or six, I believe.'

'Can you tell us the names of these people?' asked Ravenscroft, as Crabb took out his pocketbook.

'Professor Moncrief and his wife,' began the maid.

'And where do they reside?' interjected Crabb.

'In Malvern Link. They have a house overlooking the common. Then there's Miss Jayward — she is an elderly lady who lives near the railway station in Colwall. Mr Fanshawe, I believe resides in Abbey Road in Great Malvern. Mrs Tinniswood lives next door to Miss Jayward. And Colonel Mortimer — he lives opposite the church in Colwall. I think that is all.'

'You mentioned Doctor Cranbrook. Where does he reside?' asked Ravenscroft.

'He lives in the small cottage at the start of the common, in the lower village.'

'You have been most helpful to us, Gladys. We will be on our way now, if you will excuse us,' said Ravenscroft.

The maid led the way down the stairs towards the front door.

'I can assure you that you have nothing to worry about, as I said it is all just a police formality,' smiled Ravenscroft. 'Do you happen to know if Miss Fincher had any brothers, sisters, nephews or nieces?'

'The mistress never mentioned any relations. There are no family photographs in the house. No, I think she was quite alone in the world.'

'Thank you, Gladys.'

'What will become of me now, sir? Should I remain here?'

'I am afraid I cannot help you there, but until someone claims the body, or an executor of her estate comes forward, I think it might be better if you looked after the house. I am sure it will not be long before you hear something,' replied Ravenscroft, trying to sound reassuring.

'Yes, of course.'

The maid closed the front door as Ravenscroft and Crabb made their way back along the drive. As they reached the entrance, Ravenscroft turned round and looked up at the house. 'That is Miss Fincher's room, at the front left, if I am not mistaken. I tell you something, Tom, when I walked over to the sash window I noticed that the catch was not securely engaged. Interestingly, the maid said she had found it open when she found her mistress dead.'

'You mean someone could have entered the room in the night, murdered Miss Fincher, and left by the window?' asked Crabb. 'But it is two days since she was found. The maid said she had closed the window since then.'

'It is all rather confusing. The ivy is quite thick and strong, and could have assisted a murderer in climbing up the side of the house.'

'What medicines were on the bedside cabinet?'

'Beef extract, smelling salts, and one or two that had been prescribed by this Doctor Cranbrook, I presume for Miss Fincher's heart complaint. I could not detect any dangerous smells coming from inside the bottles.'

'Do you think Miss Fincher died in suspicious circumstances?' asked Crabb.

'At the moment, Tom, we have no way of telling. Certainly there were no signs that any struggle took place in the bedroom, and I suppose it could be just a coincidence that the window had not been securely fastened. Of course, Miss Fincher may well have died from natural causes. We may be reading far too much into this. Until we have visited this Doctor Cranbrook, and viewed the body, it would be foolish to make any assumptions.'

* * *

Crabb and Ravenscroft returned to the trap and made their way along the road into the centre of the village, passing by a row of houses, until the local bank and post office came into view on their right, and the railway station on their left, before they presently reached the common.

'So we return to Colwall. Do you remember when we visited the almshouses here all those years ago?' said Ravenscroft. 'That was our first case together.'

'It must have been six or seven years ago,' replied Crabb.

'We have investigated many cases together since then. Time passes by very quickly. It seems like only yesterday that I first arrived in Malvern.'

'Indeed, sir.'

'Anyway, enough of this reminiscing. According to Gladys Brotherton, this should be where we should find Doctor Cranbrook,' said Ravenscroft.

Crabb pulled up the horse outside a small cottage, where a man could be seen walking briskly up the path towards the front door.

'I trust I have the honour of addressing Doctor Cranbrook?' called out Ravenscroft.

'You do. I have just returned from visiting one of my patients. If you would give me a minute or two, I will be with you presently,' said the doctor, opening the cottage door and disappearing quickly inside before the detective could speak.

'He obviously thinks we are patients,' said Crabb.

'Rather a small premises for a country doctor. How old would you say our good doctor is?'

'Just over thirty years.'

'I would have thought mid- to late twenties. I wonder why he came to Colwall of all places to practice medicine.'

'Plenty of old people in Malvern and the surrounding districts,' offered Crabb.

'Like our Miss Fincher.'

'Sorry to have kept you,' said the doctor, opening the door again. 'Do please come in.'

The two detectives stepped into a small hall and followed the doctor into a sparsely furnished room at the front of the property.

'Would you care to take a seat, sir? Perhaps your manservant would wait outside until I have finished my consultation?'

'Fortunately, we do not require any medicinal pills or liquids, Doctor. I am Detective Inspector Ravenscroft from Ledbury, and this is Detective Sergeant Crabb.'

Cranbrook looked slightly taken aback by the detective's announcement.

'We have called upon you today in regard to one of your patients, Miss Maud Fincher.'

'Yes, Miss Fincher is, or rather, she was one of my patients. She died on Monday evening,' replied the doctor as he sat down in the chair behind the desk.

'May I ask for how long you had been treating Miss Fincher?' asked Ravenscroft.

'For about six months now; she became my patient shortly after my arrival here.'

'Why was that, Doctor? Did not Miss Fincher already have a doctor?'

'Yes, you would have thought so, but I was given to understand that Miss Fincher's doctor, a Doctor McKenzie of Malvern Link, had only recently retired, and I suppose as I had only just arrived, and appeared to be the only doctor in the village, she decided to consult with me.'

'So there are no other medical practitioners in Colwall?' asked Crabb.

'That is correct. But I don't quite understand why you are here?' asked the doctor with a puzzled expression.

'Forgive me. Shortly before Miss Fincher died, she wrote a letter to the Chief Constable in which she said that someone was trying to kill her.'

'Dear me. That sounds rather serious, I must say!'

'She mentioned someone by the name of "Old Crabbit." Do you happen to know anyone by that name?' asked Ravenscroft observing that the doctor appeared to show signs of nervousness.

'No, no, the name means nothing to me.'

'When Sergeant Crabb and I called upon Miss Fincher this morning to investigate the matter, we learned that the good lady had died suddenly on Monday evening.'

'Yes, yes, that is indeed so.'

'So you can see why we are concerned about the lady's demise.'

'Yes, of course.'

'Could you tell us what happened when you called at Miss Fincher's house?'

'It was about eight o'clock on Tuesday morning, when Miss Fincher's maid knocked on my door. She was in quite a distressed state and informed me that she had found her mistress dead that same morning. I accompanied her back to the house and entered the bedroom. Miss Fincher was lying as she had said, on the floor by the side of her bed.'

'Was she lying on her front or her back, Doctor?' interrupted Crabb.

'The lady was lying on the rug, on her front. She must have got out of her bed in the middle of the night and collapsed on the floor. I examined the body. She was quite cold and had apparently been dead for some hours. I then contacted the undertakers in Malvern Link and issued the death certificate,' replied Cranbrook, adopting a more matter-of-fact tone of voice.

'What was the cause of death?' asked Ravenscroft.

'Her heart. Miss Fincher had a weak heart. I had been treating her condition since our initial consultation.'

'Could you elaborate further, Doctor? We noticed several prescription bottles at the side of her bed.'

'Yes, I gave her beef extract to build up her constitution, and one or two tonics to relieve any pain she might incur. I also recommended plenty of rest.'

'Was she in a great deal of pain?' enquired Ravenscroft, as Crabb continued to made notes in his pocketbook.

'Not really. When elderly women reach a certain age they tend to place too much emphasis on their health, and often believe that they are far worse than they actually are.'

'You mean that Miss Fincher was prone to exaggeration?'

'Yes, you could say that.'

'How old was your patient?'

'Sixty-two, I believe.'

'Did her heart condition get worse during the six months since you have been treating her?'

'She was always complaining about heart palpitations, occasional giddiness, hot flushes, that sort of thing, but as I had only known the good lady for comparatively a short period of time I had no way of telling whether or not her condition had deteriorated.'

'How often did you visit Miss Fincher?' asked Ravenscroft.

'About every two weeks.'

'Was this at your request, or hers?'

'That was at Miss Fincher's request. Generally I would seek to reassure her that she had little to worry about, that she was to avoid all anxious situations, and I would also change her tonic — these, of course, were quite ineffectual in themselves, but nevertheless seemed to bring some kind of comfort.'

'You say, Doctor, that you thought her heart problem was not of a serious nature, and yet you stated that was the cause of her death.'

Cranbrook was nervously turning a pencil around with his fingers. 'The heart is largely a medical uncertainty. There are quite a few people who die as the result of a weakened heart, while others drop dead suddenly for no apparent reason.'

'When did you last visit Miss Fincher?'

'It was on Wednesday of last week.'

'Was there any difference in her condition then?'

'No, she seemed just the same as usual. I recommended a different tonic, that was all.'

'Did Miss Fincher ever confide in you about any other matters?'

'I don't quite understand your question, Inspector.'

'Did Miss Fincher seem worried or anxious about any other matters?'

'No.'

'She never mentioned that anyone was threatening her in any way?'

'No.'

'Did she ever mention any family members?'

'No, I was given to understand that all her relations were dead. If there were any still alive, she certainly never mentioned them to me.'

'Would death have been instantaneous?'

'There is no way of telling. I feel sure that Miss Fincher, woke in the middle of the night, got out of bed, and collapsed on the floor. She could have died straight away, or could have lain there for some time being unable to move or cry out for assistance.'

'What is your opinion, Doctor Cranbrook?'

'I would like to think that death came upon her quite suddenly,' replied Cranbrook, giving a slight smile.

'Did you make a full examination of the body?'

'No, why should I? It was quite obvious to me what the cause of death was. She was quite alone at the time of her death. There were no signs that any struggle or intrusion had taken place. There were no marks on the arms or round the throat — had there been, I would have noticed them. Now if you will excuse me, I have to call upon a patient.'

'Of course, Doctor.' Ravenscroft rose from his seat. 'Oh, just one more question — did you know that Miss Fincher was a spiritualist?'

'No.'

'Apparently she was in the habit of attending séances.'

'No, I was not aware of that,' replied Cranbrook, looking unsettled. 'She never mentioned that to me.'

'What are you views on spiritualism?'

'I don't really have any views at all. It is not something I have ever encountered. I do know that some bereaved people find reassurance in the practice. Now, I really must go, Inspector.'

'Thank you, Doctor Cranbrook. We will not detain you any further. Good day, sir.'

* * *

'Well, Tom, what do you think of our Doctor Cranbook?' asked Ravenscroft as the trap began its long climb towards the Wyche Cutting.

'He seemed very nervous, sir.'

'That is just what I thought.'

'He may have been hiding something from us,' suggested Crabb.

'Yes, although that nervousness may be his normal manner. I do find it strange, however, that such a young man, evidently starting out on his medical career, would choose to come to a small village like Colwall, where most of the patients must be visited by doctors from either Malvern or Ledbury. I would have thought that a practice in some large city might have been more financially appealing.'

'His room was quite uninviting; no books or pictures on the wall, old wooden chairs and a desk which had seen better days.'

'Yes. I do not think that his practice is in any way providing a satisfactory income, but perhaps it may grow over time.'

'We don't know what was in those bottles. He said they were tonics. He could have been giving her dangerous substances over a period of months, which might have increased the risk of her heart eventually giving out.'

'Yes, but why? Doctor Cranbrook would appear to have no reason to kill Miss Fincher, as far as I can see, although it is difficult to say at this stage in our investigations. Perhaps the good doctor is correct, and Miss Fincher died of natural causes after all. We may be jumping to conclusions. There may not be a case to investigate, but we must remember the threatening letter Miss Fincher received. I think we should pay the undertaker a visit. I would like to examine the body.'

* * *

A few minutes later, Ravenscroft and Crabb arrived in the yard of Smithers and Company, Undertakers of Malvern Link.

An elderly portly gentleman, with a large red nose and spotty complexion, dressed in a black suit, came forward to meet them.

'Mr Smithers, I presume?'

'Clarence Smithers at your service. Do please come this way, if you will. We have been expecting you all morning,' said the undertaker, sliding open a large wooden door to one side.

'Really,' said Ravenscroft, surprised, as he and Crabb followed Smithers into a large open room.

'Such a sad time for us all, but I like to think that Smithers and Company can ease the way of the deceased into the other world, while bringing a little gentle relief to those of us who have been left behind to carry on life's awesome burden.'

'Yes, quite, I wonder—' began Ravenscroft.

'The good lady lies at rest in our inner room. If you would care to follow me, gentlemen, you may view your loved one. I know it might come as rather a shock to see one's loved ones now that they are deceased, but I would urge courage. Courage is what we need in this hour of sadness,' said Smithers, rubbing his hands.

They followed the undertaker into the inner room, where a large open coffin rested on a trestle table.

'Here is the good lady, if you would care to draw near,' urged Smithers, standing to one side. 'Courage, sir, remember that, and faith.'

'Faith?' questioned Crabb.

'Why yes, faith that we will soon be reunited with our dearly departed loved ones in the next world.' Smithers blew loudly into a large spotted handkerchief.

Ravenscroft inched forwards and looked tentatively down at the elderly lady who lay shrouded inside the open coffin.

'Allow me,' said Smithers, drawing back the covering from the deceased's face. 'Perhaps you would like me to sing a hymn with you, at this time?'

'No thank you, that will not be necessary.'

'A prayer then? Yes, I think a brief prayer might be suitable upon this occasion.'

'No, thank you.'

'She looks rather elderly for her years,' remarked Crabb as he drew near.

'Death is no respecter of age. All life is but an illusion.'

'I am inclined to agree with you, Crabb. This lady has the appearance of someone well advanced in years, somewhat over eighty, I would say,' said Ravenscroft, leaning forwards and looking closely at the dead woman's face.

'Eighty-two, to be precise,' said the undertaker. 'That is what we were told.'

'Sixty-two,' corrected Ravenscroft.

'I am sure you are mistaken, sir. This lady is eighty-two. It says so on the death certificate — but I quite understand. Bereavement can sometimes cause confusion. Do not distress yourself about it. Such thoughts and feelings will quickly pass.' Smithers smiled broadly, displaying his crooked black teeth as he did so.

'Mr Smithers, I think—'

'Say no more about it. I can assure you that we will seek to enhance the good lady's appearance before the day of internment is upon us. Smithers and Company has always been known for its delicate, sympathetic responses to the desires of the bereaved. You can be confident that everything will be taken care of. You and your family will have nothing to concern yourself. Let us—'

'Mr Smithers—'

'You need have no fear. Your mother is in safe hands with Smithers and Company.'

'But this lady is not my mother,' protested Ravenscroft.

'But, but . . . I was given to understand that this dear lady is your mother.'

'I can assure you, sir, that she is not.'

'But you said you were Mr Snook when you arrived,' protested Smithers, flustered.

'I am not Mr Snook. You may have assumed that, but I can assure you that at no time have I ever claimed to be related to this dead woman,' said Ravenscroft firmly.

'So this lady, Mrs Florence Snook is not your mother?' Smithers deflated a little. 'Then who are you, sir?'

'My name is Detective Inspector Ravenscroft from the local constabulary, and this is Detective Sergeant Crabb. We are here to view the body of Miss Maud Fincher.'

'Oh, dear me! I most humbly apologise for this terrible misunderstanding. May I be so bold as to enquire what your business is with poor Miss Fincher? I have not received notification that there was anything unusual about her death. I am somewhat reluctant to let complete strangers view those who have been entrusted to our care.'

'I quite understand your position, Mr Smithers, but we are policemen, and it is our duty to inspect dead bodies if we think foul play may have been a cause of death.'

'Yes, yes, I suppose so. Doctor Cranbrook seemed perfectly satisfied with the death; a failed heart, I believe, such a common complaint, particularly amongst those over the age of sixty.'

'I hope not all that common,' said Ravenscroft, giving a brief smile.

'This way, Inspector,' said Smithers. 'Miss Fincher lies in the adjoining room.'

Ravenscroft and Crabb followed the undertaker into a smaller, darker room, where a simple wooden coffin lay on a stone slab.

'I believe this is the lady you are seeking,' said Smithers, lifting up the lid on the coffin to reveal the body.

'I believe you are correct,' said Ravenscroft, drawing near. 'Would you be so kind as to provide us with some extra light so we can inspect the corpse in more detail?'

Smithers blew his nose loudly again into his handkerchief, before reaching over to an oil lamp on a nearby table.

'Thank you,' said Ravenscroft as the undertaker turned up the flame. 'If you would give that lamp to Sergeant Crabb, I would be obliged. You may leave us now.'

'I am afraid that is quite impossible. Once a body has been entrusted to our care, it is our moral duty to see that no harm befalls it.'

'I appreciate that. If you would care to stand aside, then I have no objection to your remaining here.' Ravenscroft brought a handkerchief close to his nose.

'Certainly,' said the undertaker giving a wide grin.

During the next few minutes Ravenscroft made a detailed examination of the body, as Crabb held the oil lamp high above their heads, the silence being broken only by the deep breathing and occasional nose-blowing of Smithers the undertaker.

'Thank you, Mr Smithers, we have seen all that we need to see,' said Ravenscroft. 'We will take our leave of you.'

'Smithers and Company has been pleased to have been of service to the local constabulary. Before your departure, Inspector, I wonder if you would be kind enough to inform us as to the dead lady's next of kin, so that arrangements can be made for the burial and the furnishings for the coffin?'

'I am afraid I cannot help you with that, Mr Smithers. As far as I know Miss Fincher has no relatives.'

'Dear me, what am I to do?' asked the worried undertaker.

'The good lady may have left a will, but unfortunately we have yet to discover her executors.'

'But, but . . . where will the good lady be buried? Who will pay for the funeral? This is quite a dreadful situation, dear me,' said Smithers, gloomily shaking his head. 'This is a most unsatisfactory state of affairs.'

'Never fear, it is our intention to visit the local newspaper officer, and to ensure that a notice of Miss Fincher's demise is published as soon as possible. I am confident that it will not be too long before either someone claims the body, or we discover who holds her will. I wish you a good day.'

* * *

'Well, sir, what do you make of that?' asked Crabb as the two men climbed into the trap.

'I made a thorough examination of the body and could find no marks or bruising, or any other signs that Miss

Fincher had been attacked in any way. So it does not look as though anyone murdered her. There was also no evidence to suggest that she had been forcibly restrained. It would appear therefore that Doctor Cranbrook's conclusions as to the cause of her death were the correct ones,' said Ravenscroft.

'So you believe that she died of natural causes?'

'It would seem that way. We know that Cranbrook was treating his patient for a weak heart, and given her advanced years that would be the most likely outcome. There does remain the possibility, however, that someone deliberately entered that bedroom that night, causing Miss Fincher to suffer a fatal shock, which in turn resulted in her death, and that the intruder left the premises by climbing down the ivy on the outside of the building.'

'But if this intruder climbed up the ivy, how would he have known that the window was unsecured?' asked Crabb.

'Such an intruder may have slipped into the house, unnoticed, during the day, where he remained hidden until nightfall. He could have climbed down the ivy.'

'Why not leave by the front door?' Crabb asked.

'Perhaps he thought he would have been detected going out that way. In any case, we might be reading too much into all this. If Miss Fincher died of natural causes, and the evidence would tend to suggest this, then we have nothing to investigate,' added Ravenscroft deep in thought.

'There is that letter.'

'Yes, that is the one thing that concerns me. The day before she dies Miss Fincher sits down and writes a letter to the Chief Constable saying that she is in fear of her life from this "Old Crabbit." I don't know about you, Tom, but I will not be completely satisfied until we have tracked down this Crabbit. Only then will we be able to say whether or not Miss Fincher died of natural causes, or if this man had something to do with her death. Who was Old Crabbit — and why would he want Miss Fincher dead? Until we have answered those questions, we cannot entirely rule out foul play.'

CHAPTER THREE

FRIDAY

'Could you pass the marmalade, my dear,' requested Ravenscroft, as he and his wife were taking breakfast inside their cottage in Church Street in the Herefordshire county town of Ledbury. 'It is uncommonly good.'

'I purchased it yesterday from old Mother Johnston at the local market,' replied Lucy, passing over the jar to her husband.

'I think it most excellent. Old Mother Johnston is to be congratulated, and I suggest— no, I *command* you to purchase another jar next week,' joked Ravenscroft.

'I will endeavour to carry out your wishes,' smiled Lucy.

'I would expect nothing else.'

'Have you thought any more, Samuel, as to what you might do when you retire?' asked Lucy, knowing that she was raising a difficult subject.

'I do not care to think about it,' said Ravenscroft, spreading his toast with a large helping of the blackberry-flavoured jam.

'You could always become a private investigator, like your hero Sherlock Holmes.'

'I do not think there would be much work to be undertaken in that direction in the Three Counties. It might be alright for Holmes living in London to be kept busy by numerous clients, but out here in the countryside the possibility of people asking me to assist them would be negligible, and anyway Sherlock Holmes is not a real detective, he is but a figment of Conan Doyle's imagination,' replied Ravenscroft somewhat dismissively.

'Some retired policemen do take on other work, I believe,' suggested Lucy encouragingly.

'Yes, they run public houses or take up gardening, neither of which hold much appeal for me.'

'You could write all about your famous cases. I am sure that such a book would be read by a great many people. You might even become quite famous. People always like to read about criminals and how they are caught.'

'I don't think anyone would be interested in reading about all my old cases, and anyway I don't believe that I would be very literary,' grumbled Ravenscroft.

'Never mind. Something might come up from some unexpected quarter.'

'I doubt it.'

'At least you will have more time to spend with me and the children,' said Lucy trying to lift her husband's downcast mood.

'Richard is away most of the time at boarding school.'

'We still have Arthur. He is nearly four years old now.'

'I know, and I am thankful every day of my life for our two children,' smiled Ravenscroft. 'In fact, I think when I do retire at the end of the month, the first thing that we should do is take a holiday together.'

'Oh, Samuel, that would be so lovely. Where do you suggest?' asked an excited Lucy.

'I must admit that I have not yet actually decided where we will go. It will be a secret.'

'Do you think we can afford it?'

'I will be retiring on a pension of about three-fifths of my current salary, and we have a little put aside, so yes, I am sure we could all afford a holiday. You deserve one.'

'Perhaps we could go back to that hotel in Dinard, in Brittany — the Gandolphi, was it not?'

'Indeed it was. We shall see. Ah, I see that the notice we placed in the local newspaper yesterday, concerning Miss Fincher, has been published,' said Ravenscroft picking up the paper from the table. 'I hope someone will come forward with more information relating to the dead woman.'

'I find it very sad.'

'What is, my dear?'

'It is sad to die all alone like that, with no family around her.'

'Perhaps someone may see this and come forward.'

'What about this horrible Crabbit character?'

'I have asked Tom to make a thorough search of all the Directories for the Three Counties, to see if there is anyone of that name listed. It is quite an unusual name, so it could be easy enough to find. Of course, Directories only list the landed gentry, people with property, and those engaged in a commercial enterprise of some sort. If Crabbit is a farm labourer, or a workman, then he will not be included. Still, I am hopeful,' said Ravenscroft, buttering another piece of toast.

'There is something else you can do. You said that Miss Fincher attended séances. Why don't you go and see the people with whom she attended these séances? They might know who this Crabbit is, and they might also be able to tell you more about Miss Fincher herself,' suggested Lucy.

'I must say that does sound rather a good idea. It is a wonder I did not think of it before,' Ravenscroft teased.

* * *

'So your search of the Directories yielded nothing,' said Ravenscroft, as the trap entered the village of Colwall later that morning.

'There were a number of Crabbs, but unfortunately no Crabbits,' replied his sergeant.

'Never mind. Today, we will visit some of the members of Miss Fincher's séance group. I am hoping that they may provide us with some valuable information about the good lady.'

The trap drew up outside a small cottage near the railway station.

'We will start with Miss Jayward,' said Ravenscroft, alighting from the trap.

'She could have been Miss Fincher's confidante and friend,' said Crabb tying up the horse to a hitching post.

Ravenscroft was admiring the flowers that lined the pathway up to the front door. 'What an attractive garden.'

'Someone takes care of it,' remarked Crabb.

Before Ravenscroft could knock on the door, it was suddenly opened by a grey-haired lady, with a round cheery face and a broad smile.

'Good day to you. I presume we have the honour of addressing Miss Jayward?' said Ravenscroft, removing his hat and returning the smile.

'You do indeed.'

'I wonder if my colleague and I might take up a few minutes of your time.'

'I hope you are not from that insurance company,' frowned Miss Jayward. 'They are always calling on me. So tiresome.'

'No, I am Detective Inspector Ravenscroft from Ledbury Police Station. We hope you can tell us more about Miss Maud Fincher.'

'Yes, of course. It is such a sad business, so unexpected. I only spoke with Maud last Sunday, at the séance. You had better come in, Inspector,' said Miss Jayward, opening the door wider.

'Thank you,' said Ravenscroft as he and Crabb stepped into the hallway.

'This way, if you please.' The old lady led them into the drawing room. 'Could I offer you gentlemen some refreshment?'

'That is most kind of you,' replied Ravenscroft.

'Do take a seat, I shall not be too long. Tea?'

'That would be quite acceptable.'

Ravenscroft and Crabb seated themselves in comfortable armchairs, as their hostess disappeared from view.

'Very nice and cosy,' whispered Crabb, as they looked round the room with its thick carpet, velvet curtains, fine miniatures on the walls, and numerous Staffordshire fairings and other ornaments on the mantelpiece.

'I think Mrs Ravenscroft would be quite at home here,' remarked Ravenscroft.

A few minutes later Miss Jayward returned carrying a large tray.

'Here, do let me help you,' said Crabb, springing to his feet.

'Oh, thank you, young man. If you could place it on that small table in front of the sofa, I would be most grateful. I'm afraid I didn't catch your name.'

'Sergeant Crabb, ma'am.'

'Now, how can I help you both?'

'We are anxious to learn more about Miss Fincher. Had you known her long?' enquired Ravenscroft, as Miss Jayward took her place on the sofa.

'Not really. We have only spoken with one another during the past three or four months.'

'Miss Fincher was a recent arrival in the village?'

'Oh no, she has been living in that big house for . . . it must be nearly twenty-five years now. Or is it thirty? My memory is not as good as it was. Alas, it is the result of getting older.'

'You have lived in the village for many years?'

'Yes, I was born in this house seventy-three years ago, and after my mother, and then my father died, I lived here with my sister Amy. Unfortunately she died a few months ago.'

'I am sorry to hear it,' said Ravenscroft. 'That must have been difficult for you.'

'It was very upsetting at the time, but one soldiers on. You have to put on a brave face, you know.'

'So would you agree that Miss Fincher kept very much to herself?'

'I suppose so. I caught sight of her over the years in the village, and exchanged courtesies, but we never engaged in intimate conversation until about three months ago. Do you take milk, Inspector?'

'Yes, please. Do you know if Miss Fincher had any living relations?'

'No, I don't think she did. We never heard of anyone else staying there at Claremont, and she never spoke of anyone like that.'

'But you say you have conversed together during the past three months — why was that?' asked Ravenscroft, accepting the cup of tea.

'It was all on account of Professor Moncrief and his wife. They brought us together. Would you like tea, Sergeant?'

'Yes, thank you,' answered Crabb. 'With milk, if you please.'

'Can you elaborate further?' prompted Ravenscroft.

'It was after my late sister died. Poor Amy, she had been ill for some years. Do you know that she had never left this house during the last eight years of her illness? We often thought she would get better, but alas she did not,' said Miss Jayward sadly shaking her head. 'But these things are often sent to try us.'

'You were speaking of Professor Moncrief,' interjected Ravenscroft, anxious to steer the conversation away from his hostess's dead sister.

'Oh yes. Well, as I was saying, it was shortly after Amy died that I went to a meeting in Malvern in the Assembly Rooms, given by Professor Moncrief. He and his wife had recently moved into the area. He explained that sometimes after people had lost their loved ones, they were quite anxious to learn of ways in which they could keep in touch with them in the afterlife. Have you lost loved ones, Inspector?'

'Fortunately not recently,' answered Ravenscroft.

'What he had to say was quite moving, and very profound. All too often, people die so suddenly, before we have had time to let them know how much they mean to us. He suggested that those members of his audience who would like to know more about his mission should meet privately at his home the following week.'

'So you went to this meeting, and Miss Fincher was there?'

'She joined a month later.'

'And you meet regularly in each other's homes, I believe?' prompted Ravenscroft.

'That is so. It is quite a small group — Professor Moncrief and his wife Janet; Mrs Tinniswood, who lives next door to me,' continued Miss Jayward warming to her subject; 'Colonel Mortimer, who is such a nice man; Mr Fanshawe who is a local businessman; and of course Miss Fincher.'

'May I enquire what usually took place at these meetings?' asked Ravenscroft, curious.

'We would all sit together, usually around a table, and Professor Moncrief and his wife would then make contact with the spirit world.'

'I see,' said Ravenscroft giving Crabb a sideways glance.

'It was all so reassuring, so calming. The professor is such a wonderful man. He has bought such comfort to us all.'

'And have you made contact with your sister?' asked Ravenscroft, somewhat tentatively.

'Oh yes, Amy tells me that she is quite happy and content in her new plane of existence. You cannot imagine how comforting that is,' smiled Miss Jayward.

'I am sure.'

'We have all lost someone dear to us.'

'Can you tell me why Miss Fincher attended these séances? Was there someone in particular that she wanted to make contact with?'

'She wanted to know how her late parents were in the afterlife. I gather that they died many years ago.'

'Did Miss Fincher seem anxious to you at all?'

'Anxious? I suppose she must have been. She seemed to want their forgiveness.'

'Forgiveness for what, exactly?' asked Ravenscroft, intrigued.

'She never said, but it was all about something that happened a very long time ago. I cannot tell you more.'

'That is quite alright. Do you think that Miss Fincher was ever in fear of her own life?'

'What a strange question to ask. Maud had no enemies as far as I know. She was sometimes a little unsettled after our meetings, but that is quite normal in some people after they have suddenly been reunited with their loved ones, particularly after a long period of time.'

Suddenly there was a loud rapping at the front door.

'That will be Sarah. She usually calls on me at this time of the day. If you excuse me, Inspector,' said Miss Jayward, rising from her seat.

'Of course,' said Ravenscroft as he and Crabb stood up as their hostess left the room.

'Strange business these séances,' whispered Crabb.

'Do come in, Sarah, there is someone in here I would like you to meet,' said Miss Jayward returning to the room, closely followed by another elderly lady of a more stout stature and greying hair. 'These nice policemen are from Ledbury. They are enquiring into the death of poor Maud.'

'Oh really,' smiled the new arrival.

'Good day to you,' acknowledged Ravenscroft.

'This is Mrs Tinniswood, who lives in the next cottage. She is another member of our little group of friends.'

'I am pleased to meet you, Mrs Tinniswood,' said Ravenscroft. 'We were just on our way to call upon you. We thought you might be able to tell us something about Miss Fincher.'

'I told the Inspector that we never really spoke to Maud until she joined our group,' interjected Miss Jayward.

Mrs Tinniswood nodded in agreement.

'How long have you lived in the village?' Ravenscroft enquired.

'How long have I lived here?' repeated Mrs Tinniswood, with a puzzled expression on her face.

'You have been here for nearly twenty years.' Miss Jayward placed a comforting hand on her friend's shoulder.

'Yes, twenty years. Is it really that long?' said Mrs Tinniswood, shaking her head.

'I told the Inspector that we were all members of Professor Moncrief's little circle.'

'Oh yes, Professor Moncrief,' repeated Mrs Tinniswood with a look of recognition. 'He is such a lovely man.'

'May I ask why you attend the meetings?' asked Ravenscroft.

'Why do I attend the meetings?' repeated the elderly woman looking anxiously at her friend.

'You go because of William.'

'William? Oh yes, of course, William. He was my late husband. He died six years ago, or was it seven?'

'It was five years ago, my dear.'

'Five years, of course. I wanted to see that William was alright. I told him it would not be long before I joined him,' sighed Mrs Tinniswood, her sad voice trailing away.

'Can you tell me how Miss Fincher was at these meetings?' asked Ravenscroft, realising that perhaps all future questioning of the lady would fail to provide any additional information.

'Maud? How was Maud?' echoed a bewildered Mrs Tinniswood.

'I told the Inspector that Maud was sometimes quite anxious because of her late parents, you remember?'

'Oh yes, of course. She was quite worried about her parents.'

'Did she ever mention to you that she had been threatened in any way?'

'Oh no,' replied Mrs Tinniswood.

'Does the name "Old Crabbit" mean anything to either of you?'

'Old Crabbit,' repeated Mrs Tinniswood.

'Why, yes of course, Inspector. We know who Crabbit is,' smiled Miss Jayward.

'Yes,' said Ravenscroft hopefully.

'Silas Crabbit. He is our spirit guide.'

CHAPTER FOUR

'So this Silas Crabbit is dead, if I understand it correctly,' said Crabb as he urged the horse up the steep winding road towards the Wyche.

'Yes, according to Miss Jayward and Mrs Tinniswood, Crabbit is a spirit used by the medium to communicate with those who have passed over into a new plane of existence,' said Ravenscroft.

'You don't believe in any of that nonsense?'

'Certainly not. I believe that when you are dead, that is an end to it. All this talk of spirits in the afterlife is just pure fantasy. However both Miss Jayward and Mrs Tinniswood believe in it quite strongly.'

'Yes, but they have both lost people close to them.'

'Quite — and it seems as though Maud Fincher also believed in spiritualism, as she kept attending the meetings. And she became quite anxious at these meetings after she had communicated with her lost parents.'

'But they must have died some years ago.'

'Yes. In her letter Miss Fincher states that this Crabbit had told her that she would shortly die. Now we know that dead people cannot kill the living, so what exactly was she afraid of? Something, or someone, had clearly frightened the poor woman out of her wits at the last séance she attended. We need to know what exactly took place there, and why Miss Fincher feared for her life.'

'They were quite delightful ladies. They would not hurt anyone,' said Crabb.

'Indeed, I am inclined to agree with you. I wonder if Maud Fincher had known Crabbit in real life, and believed that he was about to return to inflict some kind of revenge on her — or was it all just a load of nonsense that played on the old woman's mind? I don't know, and that is why we are about to visit this Professor Moncrief. According to the ladies, he only arrived in the area about three or four months ago,' said Ravenscroft.

'He could be some kind of charlatan,' suggested Crabb.

'Preying on innocent and vulnerable people? That could well be the case, but we must try and keep an open mind. Let us see what the Professor has to say for himself.'

* * *

A few minutes later the trap made its way along one of the lower roads beneath the town of Great Malvern, until it reached an expanse of common land that bordered the village of Malvern Link. Here Crabb pulled the horse up outside a large rambling house built in the gothic style.

Ravenscroft pulled the large handle at the side of the door.

'Good afternoon gentlemen,' said a middle-aged man, opening the door.

'Good afternoon. Professor Moncrief?' asked Ravenscroft, observing that the man was wearing an elaborately decorated smoking jacket and plum-coloured trousers.

'It is indeed.'

'My name is Detective Inspector Ravenscroft, and this is Detective Sergeant Crabb. We are from Ledbury Police Station.'

'Ah, so you have caught me out at last. I am so sorry, I should have returned those library books two weeks ago,' joked the Professor.

'It is not about your library books, sir. We are here today because we are looking into the death of Miss Maud Fincher of Colwall,' said Ravenscroft.

'Miss Fincher dead! I was not aware that the lady was deceased. I saw her only a few days ago,' replied the Professor, the colour suddenly draining away from his face.

'She died on Monday evening. The matter was reported in the local paper.'

'I had not seen.'

'I wonder if we might come in?' asked Ravenscroft.

'Yes, yes, of course; please come this way.'

Ravenscroft and Crabb entered the property and followed their host down a tiled passageway with a number of potted plants on either side, and into a book-lined study where yet more plants sat in a number of ornamental pots on various tables.

'Please sit down. I must say, Inspector, that I am completely taken aback by your news.' Moncrief removed his spectacles and rubbed his eyes.

'I am sorry to bring you such bad news,' said Ravenscroft seating himself on a tapestry-covered sofa in the centre of the room.

'How, how, did Miss Fincher die? She seemed in perfect health last Sunday.'

'She was found on the floor by the side of her bed. We believe that her heart had failed her.'

'Dear me, how very sad.'

'We understand that she was a member of your séances group,' continued Ravenscroft, finding himself somewhat unsettled by the professor's piercing eyes. 'We have spoken with Mrs Tinniswood and Miss Jayward in this respect.'

'They are such sweet ladies. Yes, Maud was a valued member of our little circle.'

'It seems that when Miss Fincher attended your séance last Sunday afternoon she became somewhat agitated and unsettled. Can you think of what might have disturbed her?'

'No, I was not aware that she was upset in any way,' replied Moncrief a puzzled expression on his face.

'I wonder if you can tell us why Miss Fincher attended your sessions.'

'Yes, apparently her parents had died some ten or more years ago, and she thought that we might be able to make contact with them in some way.'

'And were you able to fulfil her request?'

'Yes, I am pleased to say that we did. I use the word "we" because my wife assists me in my mission.'

'You speak of a mission.'

'Yes, we see it as our Christian duty to reunite those who have been bereaved with their loved ones,' smiled Moncrief.

'How does your wife help you?' asked Ravenscroft.

'She is the medium through which the spirits speak. It is through her that the messages of love and hope are conveyed to the distressed and wanting — but you may ask her yourself,' said Moncrief as a middle-aged woman, plainly dressed, with long black hair down her back, entered the room. 'This is my wife, Janet.'

'Good day to you, Mrs Moncrief,' said Ravenscroft rising from his seat, observing the pale, strained complexion of the new arrival.

'My dear, we have some terrible news. These gentlemen are from the local constabulary. It seems that poor Maud Fincher has been found dead at the side of her bed,' said Moncrief.

'How terrible!' exclaimed his wife. 'How did Maud die?'

'Her heart gave out,' said Crabb.

'The poor soul. How absolutely terrible.'

'I was just explaining to the Inspector how we make contact with those who have departed into the afterlife,' said Moncrief.

'Yes, of course,' replied Mrs Moncrief, somewhat shyly.

'Perhaps you would be both kind enough to explain to me how this all works,' asked Ravenscroft.

'Well, we all sit round a large circular table, holding hands,' explained Moncrief. 'I call upon the spirits to come and assist us. After a few minutes of silence have elapsed, if we are fortunate, one of the spirits will speak through Janet. The spirit will be someone who is known to one of the members of our group, although sometimes other spirits may seek to intervene in the proceedings.'

'You say, "if we are fortunate?"' asked Ravenscroft, finding himself becoming more and more sceptical of the whole procedure as it was explained to him.

'Sometimes the spirits are reluctant to make contact with us.'

'Oh? And why is that?'

'On some occasions the conditions will not be conducive,' said Janet Moncrief. 'There may be a doubter in the room. The spirits always know if they are being tested.'

'Can I take you back to last Sunday afternoon? Did these spirits make contact with Miss Fincher on that occasion?' asked Ravenscroft.

'Yes,' answered Moncrief.

'You say she wanted to make contact with her long-deceased parents. Why did she want to do this?'

'I gather there was some unfinished business,' said Moncrief.

'What do you mean by that? What unfinished business?'

'I think Maud wanted to speak to her parents, to ask their forgiveness for something which had taken place a great many years ago. She had not had the opportunity to ask for that forgiveness before her parents had passed over,' said Janet Moncrief intently.

'Did she ever say what she wanted to be forgiven for?'

'No, that was never spoken of.'

'Did Miss Fincher obtain what she was seeking? Did she obtain this forgiveness?' asked Ravenscroft, intrigued.

'The spirit said that he would have to speak with his partner before such forgiveness could be granted,' said Janet Moncrief.

'How did Miss Fincher take this?'

'She was a little disturbed that she had not been given absolution, but we told her that sometimes these things took time; that the spirits are sometimes not as forthcoming as one would wish,' explained Moncrief.

Ravenscroft wondered why the Professor had first claimed upon their arrival that Maud Fincher had not been upset at this last séance, when the couple had now admitted that she had in fact been distressed by what had happened on that occasion.

'Did anything ever happen at these sessions to make Miss Fincher afraid?' asked Crabb.

'Afraid? Why no, our séances are not about fear, they are about love and reassurance,' smiled Moncrief.

'Can you tell us about Silas Crabbit,' asked Ravenscroft.

'Er, ah Silas Crabbit — how did you learn about him?' enquired Moncrief, suddenly adopting a more defensive manner.

'Miss Jayward told us that Silas Crabbit was your spirit guide.'

'Silas is just one of the spirits we make contact with,' replied Moncrief uneasily. 'There are others, of course.'

'Was it Silas Crabbit who spoke to Miss Fincher last Sunday?'

'Yes, I believe it was.'

'Did Silas Crabbit speak to other members of your group, or was he just known to Miss Fincher?'

'Oh no, Silas often speaks through me,' said Janet Moncrief.

'Forgive me, but I am a little confused. You said just now that Miss Fincher spoke with her parents last Sunday, and yet you now say that it was this Silas Crabbit?'

'I should perhaps explain, Inspector, that Silas is the guide, who speaks through my wife, on behalf of the other spirits,' said Moncrief.

'So Miss Fincher did not speak directly with her parents? This Crabbit spoke on their behalf?'

'That is correct.'

'I see. Did Silas Crabbit in any way threaten Miss Fincher?'

'Good Lord, no!' exclaimed Moncrief. 'Silas is not like that. He would never hurt anyone.'

'So is this Silas Crabbit a real person?' bewildered, Crabb scratched his head.

'It depends on what you mean by "real" Sergeant. As I have explained, Silas is merely the guide through whom we are able to communicate with those in the spirit world,' explained Moncrief.

'I think what my Sergeant is asking is whether or not this Silas Crabbit was a real person in this world, before he died?'

'Oh yes, very much so,' replied Janet Moncrief. 'Poor Silas has been with us for many years now. He first came into our lives about five years ago.'

'Did he ever mention anything about where he might have lived, or about the circumstances of his death?'

'No, I don't believe that he ever did. We did not like to pry into his life. Those in the spirit world can become a little uneasy if you question them. We knew that we had to treat Silas with respect if we were to let him into our lives,' said Moncrief.

'Did Miss Fincher ever mention where she lived before she came to Colwall?' asked Ravenscroft, changing his line of questioning.

'No, I don't think she ever spoke of that. What do you think, my dear?' asked Moncrief.

'No, she never mentioned to me where she had lived before,' confirmed his wife.

'I gather you have been here only a few months.'

'We moved to Malvern about four months ago.'

'May I ask where you lived before you came here?' asked Ravenscroft.

'I don't really see that this is at all relevant,' grumbled Moncrief.

'Shipston-on-Stour,' said Janet Moncrief.

'Thank you both for your assistance in this matter. Perhaps if you think of anything else, something that Miss Fincher may have said about her past, then you can send a message to the police station in Ledbury,' said Ravenscroft about to take his leave.

'Of course,' nodded the Professor.

'Good day, Inspector,' said Janet Moncrief coming closer to Ravenscroft and suddenly placing a hand on his shoulder. 'Forgive me, but I feel you are a kindred spirit. I sense that you have lost someone in the past, someone who was very close to you.'

'We have all lost someone at one time or another,' said Ravenscroft, somewhat startled by this unexpected intimacy.

Janet Moncrief looked directly into Ravenscroft's eyes. 'You must come to one of our séances.'

'I am sure that the Inspector is a far too busy for that,' interjected Moncrief in a reprimanding tone of voice.

Janet Moncrief removed her hand from Ravenscroft's shoulder. 'We have a gathering here next Wednesday evening at six o'clock. You would be most welcome to join us.'

'I should like that very much.'

'Here, let me see you out, Inspector,' said Moncrief, leading the way quickly out of the room.

* * *

'That was a meeting full of contradictions,' said Ravenscroft as the trap moved away from the Moncriefs' house.

'They certainly are a strange couple,' remarked Crabb. 'I could not understand half of what they said. They seemed to talk in riddles.'

'Did you notice his eyes? Rather unsettling the way he stares so.'

'Creepy,' agreed Crabb.

'When we first arrived, Moncrief said that Maud Fincher had not been disturbed by her last encounter with Silas Crabbit at the séance, but later he admitted that she had indeed been upset. Then there was all this ambiguity about Crabbit himself — sometimes they appear to be communicating with him alone, at other times it is others who speak from the spirit world. They seemed unable to give a straight answer to a straight question. I felt all the time that we were going round in circles.'

'Did you see the look that Moncrief gave his wife after she admitted that they used to live in Shipston-on-Stour?'

'So you noticed that as well. Then there was all that nonsense Janet Moncrief spoke about at the end of our meeting. I found it all rather alarming. You should have seen the look of thunder on her husband's face when she invited me to their next séance.'

'You are not going to attend?' asked Crabb.

'I do not see why not. The Moncriefs have a great deal to hide, it seems to me. Whether they truly believe they are mediums enthused with a missionary zeal to bring relief for those who have lost recent loved ones, or whether they are frauds and charlatans preying on innocent vulnerable people, I cannot decide at present. But there is only one way to find out, and that is to attend this séance and expose them for what they are.'

'It is all nonsense, if you ask me, all this talk of speaking to people who have died. It does not seem right and proper,' said Crabb.

'I am sure you are right, Tom.'

'Would you like me to come?'

'I think that might arouse suspicion,' said Ravenscroft. 'I will pretend to keep an open mind and play along with anything that happens, so as to make them believe that I am interested. If I gain their confidence, then they may let slip their guard, and we might learn more about their activities.'

'Rather you than me, sir,' smiled Crabb. 'Where are we going now?'

'We will pay a visit to the telegraph office. I want to send a telegram to the police station in Shipston to see if they can provide us with any information regarding the Moncriefs when they lived there, and also if they know anything about this Silas Crabbit.'

'You think Crabbit was a real person?'

'I believe so. I cannot see that he is just a figment of the Moncriefs' imaginations. After that, we will pay a visit to another member of the group, Colonel Mortimer. I am afraid the poor horse will have to climb the hill to Colwall again on our way back home.'

* * *

Later that day Ravenscroft and Crabb stood outside an old cottage, which was situated opposite Colwall Church.

After waiting for over a minute, and with repeated knockings, the detectives were on the point of leaving when suddenly the door was opened by an elderly gentleman, wearing a pair of stained trousers, and an old coat that had probably outlived its usefulness some ten years ago.

'Damn it, man, can't a fellow find peace and quiet in his home anymore!'

'I am sorry for the intrusion, but am I addressing Colonel Mortimer?' asked Ravenscroft, somewhat taken aback by the outspoken remark.

'Of course you are, otherwise you would be somewhere else,' he grumbled.

'My name is Detective Inspector Ravenscroft, and this is Detective Sergeant Crabb. We are from Ledbury Police Station.'

'That's as may be — what do you want? I'm busy.'

'It is concerning the death of Miss Maud Fincher.'

'Yes, I read about it in the local newspaper. Bad business. Don't see what it is to do with me. You must ask others. Now good day to you,' said the Colonel briskly, attempting to close the door in the detectives' faces.

Ravenscroft placed his hand on the door. 'It concerns Silas Crabbit.'

'Crabbit? How do you know about that?' asked Mortimer.

'We have just spoken with Professor Moncrief.'

The Colonel looked hard at Ravenscroft, and even harder at Crabb, before running his fingers over his moustache and adding, rather grudgingly, 'I suppose you had better come in, then.'

'Thank you, sir. We are most obliged.'

'You will have to take me as you find me,' said Mortimer, throwing open the door and indicating to the two detectives that they were to enter.

They stepped into a dingy hall, where numerous piles of books were stacked up against the walls, below a number of faded photographs of people in military uniform.

'This way.' Mortimer led them into a room where the smell of a recently smoked cigar hung stale in the air, and where a large collection of newspapers and other debris lay scattered on various chairs and tables.

'Sit down there,' said the Colonel, removing a pile of papers from a worn leather sofa and throwing them on to the floor.

'Thank you, sir,' said Ravenscroft, accepting the seat.

'You will have to excuse the state of the place,' said Mortimer adopting a more conciliatory tone. 'Things have not been the same since my wife died just over a year ago. I sent the servants away, as I had no need for them.'

'I am sorry to hear of the death of your wife,' said Ravenscroft, realising that he would need to be diplomatic with his questioning, for fear of alienating his host.

'Daphne was my life, you know,' said Mortimer sadly, sinking down into a large armchair that lay before a smouldering fire.

'It must be hard for you.'

'It has been damned hard.'

'You were in the army?'

'Yes, served in India and Afghanistan. Hard time we had of it, I can tell you. It wasn't all tea in the club house and billiards, you know.'

'I am sure it wasn't,' said Ravenscroft.

'Still, I don't suppose you want to hear all about that. Those days are long gone and done with. I retired from the army ten years ago. I was at a bit off a loss at first. I didn't quite know what to do with myself. Then we came here to Colwall. Sleepy old place, but that suited us. People left us alone while they got on with their own business. Everything was going along quite fine until poor Daphne died.'

'We understand that both you and Miss Fincher were members of Professor Moncrief's spiritualist group?' asked Ravenscroft, attempting to steer the conversation back to the matter in hand.

'Yes.'

'Can you tell me how you came to join the group?'

'I picked up the paper one day and saw that Moncrief had recently arrived in the town and that he was giving a talk on spiritualism at the Assembly Rooms, so I decided to go along and see what it was all about. Then Moncrief invited two or three of us into his home to attend one of his séances. I was very sceptical at first, thinking that the fellow was a mountebank of some kind, but I decided to keep an open mind. I was quite taken aback by what I found.'

'Why was that, Colonel?' asked Ravenscroft.

'At that first meeting, Moncrief's wife, Janet, went into some kind of trance. Then she began to speak in a strange voice. I was quite alarmed. But then this voice — it was a man's voice — said he had been speaking with my wife Daphne, and that she was concerned that I was neglecting to take care of myself. This spirit guide seemed to know everything about me — Daphne's name, her age, and that we had lived in India for some years, and lots more. It did not seem at all possible, but the evidence seemed to prove that there was an afterlife. I was reassured to speak with my wife again, to ask her questions, and to know that everything was alright with her.'

'So you have been attending the séances ever since?'

'Whenever I can. I quite look forward to them.'

'And Miss Fincher, why do you think she attended these meetings?'

'Apparently she had lost both her parents, many years ago, and was troubled because she had not sought their forgiveness beforehand.'

'Did she ever say what this forgiveness was for?'

'No, bit of a mystery, I suppose. She didn't want to tell us, but I gather she was quite worried by it. It was plain for all to see that some kind of guilt had hung over her for a great many years. Perhaps by attending our little meetings she was seeking to atone for her misdeeds.'

'That is all very interesting,' remarked Ravenscroft. 'Can you tell us about the meeting that took place last Sunday?'

'I'll try. What do you want to know?' the Colonel reached out for a log and threw it on to the fire.'

'Did Miss Fincher make contact with her parents?'

'Yes, and again she asked for their forgiveness, and when it wasn't given she became quite upset, so much so that she left the meeting rather abruptly.'

'Why do you think she was upset?'

'I've just told you, man, it was because that Crabbit intervened as usual, damn the fellow!'

'Silas Crabbit? The one who speaks through Janet Moncrief?'

'That's about it. He can be a bit of a swine when things aren't going his way.'

'I'm sorry, I don't quite understand,' said Ravenscroft, puzzled.

'Old Crabbit is a prickly sort of character. If you ask him too many questions, which he does not like, then he will clam up. He's done that once or twice with me when I've been communicating with my poor Daphne. He just clams up and refuses to say anything else.'

'And did this happen with Miss Fincher last Sunday?'

'Yes. The poor woman had just made contact with her mother, then Crabbit intervened and that was that. That is why she left.'

'Did Crabbit threaten her in any way?' asked Crabb.

'No. She pleaded with him to let her continue speaking with her mother, and he cut her off. That is what upset her.'

'I presume that Silas Crabbit was once a living man. Did he ever mention anything about his life on earth before his death, such as where he might have lived or how he might have died?'

'No, Crabbit keeps everything to himself.'

'Has Professor Moncrief ever asked you for any kind of financial remuneration for his services?'

'I may have helped out once or twice in the past,' admitted Mortimer.

'Can you elaborate further, Colonel?'

'No, I can't. That is my business,' said Mortimer, resuming his former assertive manner. 'It is no concern of yours.'

'I understand,' said Ravenscroft deciding that he had probably outstayed his welcome. 'Oh, the Moncriefs have invited me to attend a midweek séance at their house next Wednesday evening. May I enquire if you will be there?'

'Of course I will. I'll see you out,' grumbled the old soldier, shuffling his way out of the room.

* * *

'So we now know that the Moncriefs have taken money from Colonel Mortimer, although he was not prepared to say exactly what the money was for,' said Ravenscroft, as the trap left the village and began its journey along the narrow lanes towards Ledbury.

'That means that they have probably taken money from other members of the group.'

'I am sure of it — but I wonder if people are making small donations for the service that the Moncriefs are providing, or are there larger sums of money involved here? Are the Moncriefs missionary philanthropists bringing reassurance and guidance to those who have been bereaved, or are they unsavoury individuals preying on vulnerable people? Perhaps we may be able to answer those questions after I have attended their next séance.'

'That Crabbit sounds a nasty character,' remarked Crabb.

'Yes, although the accounts of that last séance seem to differ between each person we speak with. According to Mrs

Tinniswood and Miss Jayward, Maud Fincher was just anxious, whereas the Moncriefs cannot seem to agree on her state of mind, and Colonel Mortimer tells us that she was quite distressed when Crabbit would not let her speak with her dead mother, so much so that she left the meeting early. Whichever is the true account, we know that Miss Fincher was so upset by the encounter that she believed that Crabbit was about to kill her. I must say I agree with you, Tom, when you say that Crabbit sounds an unpleasant character. He seems to manipulate events to his own favour, preventing or allowing the members to communicate with their loved ones, while giving nothing away about himself. I have now come to the conclusion that this Crabbit is an invented character.'

'What do you mean, sir?'

'It seems to me that the Moncriefs are using Crabbit as a means of controlling the meetings — but what is the purpose behind it all?'

'Money?'

'Yes, Tom, it always seems to come down to money.'

CHAPTER FIVE

MONDAY

The following Monday morning Ravenscroft made his way to the police station in Ledbury, deep in thought about the events of the previous week. It had been a quiet weekend with no progress in the investigation into Maud Fincher's death. The telegram he had sent to the police station in Shipston-on-Stour requesting information about the activities of the Moncriefs had yet to receive a reply, and despite the posting of his notice in the local newspaper, no one had come forward to claim the dead woman's body. He was powerless to do anything until events took a new course. In all probability he would have to wait until he was able to attend the séance at the Moncriefs' house on Wednesday evening. Several times during the past few days he had asked himself whether this case was worth his time and attention. Perhaps Maud Fincher had died of natural causes, and there had been no foul play at all. After all, the only person who had possibly threatened the good woman had been Silas Crabbit, and he had probably never existed in real life, being merely a figment of the Moncriefs' imagination.

'Good morning, Tom. I trust you and the family had a good weekend,' said Ravenscroft as he entered the police station.

'Yes, thank you, sir — and you?' replied Crabb, looking up from a large ledger on the counter.

'Yes, indeed, although I cannot help thinking about this case all the time. Do you consider that we might be wasting our time with it?'

'It is difficult to say. There is no evidence to suggest that Maud Fincher was harmed by anyone, but there was that letter and the unlocked window. Oh, this came for you in the morning post,' said Crabb, retrieving a letter from beneath the counter.

'Let us hope it is some good news,' said Ravenscroft opening the envelope and reading its contents. 'It is from Clarence Smithers, the undertaker in Malvern Link. Apparently someone has come forward to claim the body — a Mr Marcus Snaith, from Maltravers, Wells and Snaith, Solicitors, of Belle Vue Terrace, Great Malvern. Furthermore, Smithers informs us that the funeral is to take place at St James the Great, Colwall, tomorrow morning at ten thirty. Good news, indeed. Perhaps we can now make some progress with this case.'

'I take it we shall be paying this Mr Snaith a visit?' asked Crabb, closing the ledger.

'You guess correctly. Harness the horse, Tom, and we will be on our way to Malvern.'

* * *

Later that morning, Crabb and Ravenscroft made their way along Belle Vue Terrace, at the top of the town, after first leaving their horse and trap in the care of one of the nearby inns.

'Ah, here we are,' said Ravenscroft, reaching a large, heavily studded doorway. He read the faded brass plaque at the side of the entrance. '"Maltravers, Wells and Snaith, Solicitors at Law." You never know what businesses are waiting to be discovered above the shops and banks, until you look closer.'

Ravenscroft pushed open the door, and the two detectives found themselves in a gloomy passageway, with peeling paper on the walls and a threadbare makeshift carpet on the floor.

'It looks as though we are in for a bit of a climb,' remarked Crabb, as Ravenscroft began to ascend the old wooden staircase situated at the far end.

Reaching the first-floor landing, Ravenscroft paused to recover his breath, as he looked upwards at an even narrower flight that stretched upwards before them. 'There must be quite a number of clients over the years who have given up in the endeavour of trying to reach them, or have died in the attempt.'

'Steeper than the Beacon,' agreed Crabb. 'Perhaps they only undertake home visits.'

Gaining the upper landing, Ravenscroft pushed open the door at the top, and entered a small office, where a clerk sat hunched over a pile of papers.

'Good day. Are these the offices of Maltravers, Wells and Snaith?' said Ravenscroft, somewhat breathless.

'Yes they are, sir,' sniffed the grey-haired clerk as he rose slowly from his stool.

'We would like to speak with Mr Snaith, if you will,' said Crabb.

'I am afraid Mr Snaith is very busy at the moment. Could you possibly come back later this afternoon, gentlemen? I am sure that Mr Snaith will see you then,' said the clerk dismissively, before resuming his seat.

'It is imperative that we see Mr Snaith now, on a matter of the greatest urgency,' said Ravenscroft, not wishing to make the climb twice in one day.

'That's as may be, but Mr Snaith cannot be disturbed. He is working on some important papers at present and has left strict instructions that he cannot be interrupted under any circumstances.'

'Will you kindly break into Mr Snaith's deliberations and inform him that Inspector Ravenscroft and Sergeant

Crabb are here to see him about the estate of the late Miss Maud Fincher,' replied Ravenscroft in a firm voice.

'Oh, Miss Fincher, you say?'

'That is correct. The late Miss Maud Fincher of Colwall. We understand from the undertaker that your firm has some interest in this case.'

'If you will wait here, gentlemen, I will see if you can be accommodated,' said the clerk, rising from his stool and quickly disappearing through a door.

'Place could do with a clear-out,' remarked Crabb, looking at the piles of papers, ledgers and dusty old books that seemed to occupy most of the room.

'Ah, but then you never know when one of these old papers might be needed. He who discards without thought often lives later to regret his folly,' said Ravenscroft.

'Mr Snaith can spare you a few moments of his precious time,' sniffed the clerk, returning to the room. 'This way, gentlemen, if you will.'

The two detectives followed the clerk down a dark airless corridor until they reached a door at the far end.

'Enter!' called out a voice from within, in response to the clerk's gentle tap.

Ravenscroft and Crabb entered a small room, where a stern-looking man sat writing behind a desk.

'Take a seat,' instructed the writer, without looking up from his work.

'Mr Snaith, I believe?' said Ravenscroft, seating himself before the desk.

'I am Marcus Snaith. I would be obliged if you would conduct your business with us as quickly as possible, as I am very busy at the present time,' replied Snaith in an offhand manner.

'I am Detective Inspector Ravenscroft from the police station at Ledbury, and this is my colleague, Detective Sergeant Crabb. We are looking into the death of Miss Maud Fincher,' said Ravenscroft.

Snaith paused in his writing and looked cautiously across at Ravenscroft. 'I was not aware there was anything to investigate. The poor lady died of heart failure, I believe.'

'That is correct, Mr Snaith, but we have reason to believe that the good lady's death may have been the result of extraneous circumstances,' replied Ravenscroft, knowing from past experience that he would need to choose his words carefully when dealing with a member of the legal profession.

'Extraneous circumstances? What extraneous circumstances?' asked Snaith, leaning back in his chair.

'The day before she died Miss Fincher wrote a letter to the Chief Constable, in which she feared for her life.'

'Did she? But I have copy of the death certificate, signed by Doctor Cranbrook, which states quite clearly that Miss Fincher died of natural causes.'

'That is correct,' admitted Ravenscroft.

'Then I do not see what there is to interest the police in this case,' said Snaith dismissively.

'We have to follow all avenues. I understand that you are Miss Fincher's solicitor?'

'Indeed, yes, but I have to tell you that Maltravers, Wells and Snaith have had no business with Miss Fincher, except for the drawing up of her will.'

'May I ask when that was?'

'Miss Fincher instructed us some fifteen years ago, I believe,' replied Snaith, shuffling through some documents on his desk. 'Yes, here we are. She made the will in August 1880, with my partner Septimus Maltravers. The will was witnessed by two of our clerks and appoints the firm as executors.'

'Then perhaps I might have a word with Mr Maltravers. I would be interested to know if any relations or friends were present when the will was signed.'

'I am afraid that is not possible.'

'Why?'

'Mr Maltravers died ten years ago,' replied Snaith with a degree of finality.

'And Mr Wells?' asked Ravenscroft.

'He retired to Weymouth some five years ago.'

'May I have a look at the will?'

'Certainly not. The will is a private document drawn up between Miss Fincher and Maltravers, Wells and Snaith. It would be highly unethical of me to break such a confidence,' pronounced Snaith, once more reverting to his dry formal tone of voice.

'But Miss Fincher is now deceased, and consequently the contents of the will are in the public domain,' suggested Ravenscroft, aware that he was treading on thin ice.

'Not until probate is granted. I would be failing in my duty if I were to allow the world and his wife access to matters which don't concern them.'

'But this is a police matter, and I can assure you that it concerns us a great deal. We are faced with a possible murder investigation, and we need to know everything we can about Miss Fincher,' insisted Ravenscroft.

'This is totally unacceptable. This will is still private,' declared Snaith forcefully.

'I am afraid Mr Snaith that if you are unable to tell us the contents of Miss Fincher's will, then it will become a police matter, and we would have to ask you to accompany us to the police station for further questioning. Now I know that you are very busy man, and I am sure that you would not want it to come to that,' said Ravenscroft trying to sound as determined as he could.

Snaith glared for a moment, and then wriggled uncomfortably in his chair, before speaking. 'Very well, but I must register a strong note of disapproval.'

'It has been noted.'

Snaith said nothing as he adjusted his spectacles on the end of his long nose and unfolded the document on the desk before him.

'Well?' enquired Ravenscroft after a period of silence had elapsed.

'Miss Fincher makes one or two small bequests — the sum of fifty pounds to Maltravers, Wells and Snaith, in the way of remuneration for their legal and executorial services, the sum of two hundred pounds to Doctor Barnardo's orphans—'

'Yes, we believe that Miss Fincher was on the local committee,' interjected Ravenscroft, remembering that the Chief Constable had mentioned that his wife and the deceased had both been involved with this philanthropic institution.

'Very commendable,' muttered Snaith. 'The rest of the estate passes to her cousin, one Rupert Fincher.'

'We were given to understand that Miss Fincher had no living relatives,' said Ravenscroft, taken aback by this unexpected news.

'Your understanding is incorrect. There is a cousin. It is here in black and white.'

'Does it say where this Rupert Fincher resides?'

'Yes, apparently he lives in the town of Cirencester.'

'Cirencester,' remarked Crabb.

'A small town in Gloucestershire on the edge of the Cotswolds,' said Snaith, adopting the tone of a schoolmaster speaking down to one of his pupils.

'Yes, I have visited it before. May I ask if you have yet made contact with this gentleman?' asked Ravenscroft.

'We have telegraphed the said gentleman, and I have this morning received a reply, in which he states that he will be arriving in town tomorrow morning in time for the funeral.'

'Good, then we look forward to having a word with Mr Fincher. Perhaps he will be able to tell us some more about his cousin's history,' said Ravenscroft. 'Mr Snaith, could you give us an approximation as to the value of Miss Fincher's estate?'

Snaith gave Ravenscroft a strong look of disapproval. 'That is not possible.'

'Why is that?'

'We would need to contact the local bank to see what assets Miss Fincher had deposited there,' replied Snaith sourly.

'But I am sure you must have done that already,' suggested Ravenscroft.

'Good day to you, Inspector,' said Snaith picking up his pen and gathering up some papers before him.

Without another word, the two detectives left the room.

* * *

As Ravenscroft opened the door on to Belle Vue Terrace, he was surprised to discover Doctor Cranbrook about to enter the building.

'Good morning to you, Doctor,' said Ravenscroft.

'Er . . . good morning to you, Inspector,' replied the doctor, somewhat taken aback.

'We have just been paying Mr Snaith a visit. He seemed in perfect health to me.'

'My business with Mr Snaith is of a personal nature,' said Cranbrook, giving Ravenscroft a look of disapproval. 'Now if you will excuse me.'

'We will not detain you.' Ravenscroft stepped aside to let the medical man enter.

Cranbrook nodded and quickly walked along the passageway and up the stairs.

'I wonder what business Cranbrook has with Snaith,' said Ravenscroft, closing the door behind him as he stepped out into the street.

'He seemed rather anxious not to engage us in conversation,' said Crabb.

'Yes. And what did you make of our Mr Snaith?'

'He was a miserable old so-and-so,' remarked Crabb, as the two men walked back along Belle Vue Terrace.

'He certainly did not want us to see that will, nor was he prepared to tell us the value of Miss Fincher's estate. It does seem that throughout my professional career, when I have had the misfortune to encounter members of the legal profession, I have always found myself backed into a corner, trying to defend my actions while attempting to extract answers from straightforward questions,' moaned Ravenscroft.

'Oh, I don't know, they are not all like that. Mr Midwinter from Ledbury has always been most accommodating.'

'You are right, Tom. I have become rather too cynical and judgemental in my old age. Perhaps it is right that I retire and made room for younger men with more open minds.'

'It is a wonder they do any business at all, in view of the long climb to their chambers and the depressing surroundings,' said Crabb, changing the subject.

'Yes, but these firms have long histories, and they accumulate vast collections of legal papers, which although they may lie dormant for a number of years, are eventually needed when their clients die, move house, or wish to check on their investments.'

'I suppose so,' admitted Crabb.

'At least we have now learned that Miss Fincher was not entirely alone in this world. A cousin, Rupert Fincher, now stands to inherit. He arrives tomorrow for the funeral. We will need to question him. Let us hope that he may provide us with some information concerning his late cousin, which might be of assistance to us in the solving of this case.'

CHAPTER SIX

TUESDAY

'It will be interesting to see who attends Maud Fincher's funeral today,' remarked Ravenscroft the following morning, as he and Crabb walked along the narrow lane that would take them to the Church of St James the Great in the parish of Colwall.

'Rupert Fincher?'

'Yes. I would hope to have words with the said gentleman. He may provide us with valuable information regarding the past life of his cousin before she came to Colwall. From what the Moncriefs have told us, something seems to have happened to her all those years ago, something so bad that it estranged her from her parents and made her leave and settle in Colwall. Whatever it was, Maud Fincher seems to have regretted it for the rest of her life.'

'Good day to you, Inspector.'

Ravenscroft turned round to see that the speaker was Professor Moncrief.

'Good day to you, Professor Moncrief. Mrs Moncrief,' replied Ravenscroft raising his hat.

'A sad day for us all, I am afraid,' said Janet Moncrief.

'Indeed so,' replied Ravenscroft courteously indicating that the professor and his wife should go before them.

'Thank you,' smiled Moncrief.

'I hope you are looking forward to our little meeting tomorrow night?' smiled Janet Moncrief.

'Of course.'

Ravenscroft and Crabb watched as the couple walked onwards.

'Rather you than me, sir,' said Crabb. 'I don't hold with all this nonsense of trying to speak to the dead.'

'I must try and keep an open mind concerning these matters, if I am to learn more about those two. If they are charlatans, out to appropriate money from vulnerable souls, then I need to expose them. They may also have made up this Crabbit spirit guide as a means of frightening Maud Fincher into an early death.'

The two men continued their walk in silence, until they finally drew nearer to the church. Suddenly Ravenscroft reached out and stopped Crabb.

'Wait here a moment, Tom. It looks as though our Professor is having some kind of altercation with one of the mourners.'

'Both men seem to be raising their voices,' added Crabb.

'Not the conduct one would expect at a funeral service. I wonder who that gentleman is?'

Moncrief looked briefly in Ravenscroft's direction, and then disappeared inside the church. The other man looked down at the ground for a few seconds before following on.

'That was all very interesting. We must have words with that gentleman after the internment. Let us take a seat at the back of the church so that we can observe all those who attend,' said Ravenscroft, pushing open the old wooden door and entering the building.

'The Moncriefs have taken their seats,' said Crabb, as the two men sat down in one of the pews.

'And behind them, I think I see Colonel Mortimer, Miss Jayward and Mrs Tinniswood, and that other gentleman we saw just now. I wonder if he is perhaps Mr Fanshawe. He was mentioned to us as being another member of the Moncriefs' group.'

'There are not many people here,' remarked Crabb, looking around the Early English-style church.

'No. The rather large lady sitting in the front pew on the other side of the aisle could very well be the Chief Constable's wife. Then there are two or three local people who look as though they have decided to attend, either out of respect or curiosity.'

'Who is the woman in black sitting two or three rows back?' asked Crabb.

'Is that not Gladys Brotherton? No doubt paying her last respects to her mistress.'

'She will now need to seek new employment.'

'Perhaps Rupert Fincher might retain the old house, and have need of her services,' suggested Ravenscroft.

'All rise!' called out the vicar.

Ravenscroft turned to see the undertaker, Smithers, enter the church, followed by a coffin supported by a number of black-coated men.

'Still no sign of Rupert Fincher,' whispered Crabb as the procession made its way up the aisle towards the altar. 'Unless he's one of the pallbearers.'

'Please sit, ladies and gentlemen,' indicated the clergyman. 'We are all here today to remember before God Maud Alice Fincher, late of this parish. Therefore we welcome you into this house of prayer, that here today you may know the peace of Christ in communion with all God's faithful servants. I have no doubt that it would have been of great comfort to the dear lady to see that so many of her friends have joined us for this occasion.'

'Not that many,' muttered Crabb.

'Miss Fincher was a highly respected member of the local community, and I am given to understand that she was a prominent member of the local fundraising committee for Doctor Barnardo's children's homes, a charity which is represented here today. Miss Fincher has been a loyal and faithful supporter of this church for over twenty years, and she will be sadly missed—'

Suddenly the service was interrupted by the loud opening of the church door.

Everyone turned round to look as a young, smartly attired gentleman entered the church, closely followed by Marcus Snaith, the solicitor.

'Please excuse our late arrival,' said the young man, striding up the main aisle of the church and taking a seat at the front. 'Please proceed.'

'Rupert Fincher, I have no doubt,' whispered Ravenscroft. 'Talk about making a last-minute dramatic entrance.'

'And that miserable solicitor, Snaith,' added Crabb.

'As I was saying, Miss Maud Fincher will be sadly missed by all her friends . . .'

* * *

Ravenscroft and Crabb watched from the edge of the churchyard as the burial service drew to a close.

'May God our Father forgive us our sins and bring us to the eternal joy of his kingdom where dust and ashes have no dominion. Amen.' The vicar made the sign of the cross over the open grave.

Rupert Fincher moved forwards, picked up a handful of earth, and threw it on to the coffin.

The mourners drifted away one by one, but not before Rupert Fincher had personally conversed with each person, as Marcus Snaith looked on in silence.

'Tom, go and see if you can ask Mr Fanshawe — if that is he we saw arguing with Moncrief — if he would be kind enough to remain behind, so that I may have a few words with him,' instructed Ravenscroft. 'I am going to try to speak with Mr Fincher.'

Crabb moved away, as Ravenscroft waited for Snaith and Fincher to leave the churchyard.

'Mr Snaith,' said Ravenscroft, addressing the solicitor.

'Ravenscroft,' acknowledged Snaith grudgingly.

'Mr Fincher, I wonder if I might have a few words with you,' continued Ravenscroft. 'My name is Detective Inspector Ravenscroft and I am making enquiries regarding the death of your late cousin.'

'Well, I . . .' stuttered the young man somewhat taken aback by the detective and looking across at the solicitor for guidance.

'Really, Ravenscroft, this is neither the place nor the time,' reprimanded Snaith. 'Show some respect, man.'

'I stand corrected,' said Ravenscroft. 'Perhaps I could make an appointment to speak with Mr Fincher this afternoon.'

'Totally uncalled for,' snapped the solicitor.

'That is alright, Mr Snaith. I am happy to oblige the Inspector. I am staying at the Abbey Hotel in Great Malvern.'

'Perhaps I might speak with you there? Would three o'clock this afternoon be acceptable?' asked Ravenscroft.

'Rupert, you don't have to speak with this man,' interjected Snaith, beginning to turn away.

'It is a matter of the greatest importance,' emphasised Ravenscroft.

'Yes, yes, of course,' said Fincher.

'Thank you, sir,' said Ravenscroft raising his hat. 'Good day to you. I am sorry for your loss.'

Fincher moved away without saying anything, as Snaith gave Ravenscroft a withering look.

'Mr Fanshawe, this is Inspector Ravenscroft,' said Crabb, as Ravenscroft walked up to the two men.

'Your sergeant here said that you wanted a word concerning Miss Fincher. I don't really see how I can help you,' said the sandy-haired, moustached man.

'Indeed. We are given to understand that both you and Miss Fincher were members of Professor Moncrief's circle,' said Ravenscroft.

'That is so. Why do you ask?'

'It is just that we have some concerns regarding Miss Fincher's death.'

'Concerns? What concerns? I thought Miss Fincher died of natural causes.' Fanshawe sounded perplexed.

'I understand that you were present at the last meeting that Miss Fincher attended, the Sunday before last,' said Ravenscroft, deciding it would be better to ignore the last question.

'Yes, that is so, but I still don't see what all this is about.'

'Could you tell us how Miss Fincher seemed at that meeting?'

'She was decidedly upset, so much so that the good lady left early.'

'Can you remember why she was upset, Mr Fanshawe?'

'Miss Fincher was trying to make contact with her lost parents, and that damned spirit guide would not let her.'

'Silas Crabbit?' asked Crabb.

'Yes, how do you know about him?'

'We have spoken with the Moncriefs already,' answered Ravenscroft.

'I see. Well, I can tell you now that those scoundrels were playing her like a violin.'

'When did you first met the Moncriefs?' asked Ravenscroft.

'It was about three or four months ago. I had just lost my wife, Agnes, and I attended a meeting in the Winter Gardens, after which a group of us visited the Moncriefs in their home. I was feeling lonely and sad after my wife's death.'

'That is quite understandable,' sympathised Ravenscroft.

I was clutching at straws. Do you know what it is like to lose someone you have cared for? No, I can see that you do not. It is a damned unhappy situation. I thought the Moncriefs could offer some comfort, some relief, but I realise now that I was very vulnerable. They took advantage of my situation.'

'Could you tell me how?'

'They led me on through that Crabbit, gave me false hope, but after a time I saw through their spurious antics. I saw how they were preying on innocent people who had lost loved ones. It was despicable.'

'Did the Moncriefs ever ask you for money?' asked Crabb.

'Yes. They said they wanted to build a new spiritualist church in Malvern where people would come and pray and make contact with their loved ones.'

'So they asked you for a donation?' continued Ravenscroft.

'I'm a builder by trade. They wanted me to build them a church near Link Common, at my expense. That is when I realised that they were scoundrels, and I became determined to expose them for what they are.'

'Did they ask you for money directly?'

'No, they just wanted me to build that wretched thing.'

'Do you know if they approached other members of your circle with requests for money?'

'I would not be surprised, although I have no evidence of this.'

'You said just now, Mr Fanshawe, that you became determined to expose the Moncriefs. How do you intend doing that, sir?'

'Why, by continuing to attend their little séances, so that I can catch them out one day, and expose them for what they are. '

'That is very commendable,' remarked Crabb.

'I could not help noticing that you and Professor Moncrief were exchanging words before you went into the church. Could you tell me what all that was about?' asked Ravenscroft.

'Moncrief has become concerned that I am not going to carry out his request to build the spiritualist church in Malvern. He wondered why I had not started the project. I told him that I was a very busy man and that I needed more time to plan the enterprise. He then accused me of not being a true follower. I told him that I would not be rushed into these matters. He became annoyed and walked away.'

'I see.'

‘All I need is time to expose Moncrief and his wife for what they are. When I have enough evidence you will be the first to hear about it. Now if you will excuse me, I have urgent business to attend to later this morning in Worcester,’ said Fanshawe.

‘Thank you for your time, Mr Fanshawe. It may interest you to know that I have been invited to attend the séance at the Moncriefs’ house tomorrow evening.’

‘Then I will see you there, Inspector, and perhaps we will both be able to bring these charlatans to account.’

Ravenscroft said nothing as the builder strode down the lane.

‘He was quite forthcoming,’ remarked Crabb.

‘Yes, there is clearly no love lost between our Mr Fanshawe and the Moncriefs.’

‘It certainly seems that the Moncriefs are after people’s money.’

‘Maybe, although interestingly Fanshawe could not confirm that the Moncriefs had asked others for donations towards their new church. They might be quite genuine in their desire to establish a spiritualist church here in Malvern.’

‘You don’t believe that, sir?’ asked Crabb.

‘Time will tell, Tom. Time will tell.’

* * *

Later that afternoon, Ravenscroft and Crabb walked underneath the Abbey Gateway in Malvern, and up the steps of the adjoining imposing Abbey Hotel.

‘Can I help you, sir?’ asked the clerk behind the large wooden counter.

‘I have an appointment to see Mr Rupert Fincher,’ said Ravenscroft.

‘The gentleman is waiting for you in the lounge.’

‘Thank you.’

The two detectives made their way along the corridor.

As Ravenscroft turned into the lounge he was disappointed to see that Marcus Snaith was sitting in a large armchair next to Rupert Fincher.

'Mr Fincher, it is very good of you to see us, especially in the present circumstances,' said Ravenscroft, knowing that he would have to choose his words wisely in the presence of the solicitor.

'I hardly knew my cousin,' said Fincher hesitantly.

'Nevertheless, it is not pleasant to lose a relation, no matter how distant,' said Ravenscroft as he and Crabb sat down on the sofa before the roaring fire.

'We would appreciate it, Inspector, if you came quickly to the point,' interjected Snaith. 'Both my client and I are busy men. There is a lot to finalise in the next few days.'

'Of course. I promise that we will not detain you more than is necessary. We understand that your cousin once lived in Cirencester.'

'Yes,' replied the young man.

'Where would that be, sir?'

'The Fincher family home is situated near the entrance to Great Park,' said Snaith answering for his client.

'And how long have you lived there Mr Fincher?' asked Ravenscroft, trying to ignore the solicitor.

'Since I was a boy.'

'That was after your cousin left?'

'No, not exactly.'

'Could you explain, sir?' prompted Ravenscroft.

'My cousin left Cirencester about twenty-five or thirty years ago, before I was born. When her parents died, my parents inherited the property,' answered Fincher, moving uneasily in his chair.

'Look, I don't see what all this has to do with your investigations into Miss Fincher's death,' interrupted Snaith. 'This was all such a long time ago. It is hardly relevant now.'

'Why did she not inherit the property, as the only child of the owners?'

'I was too young to know the details, I am afraid.'

'There are plenty of examples of brothers inheriting property rather than daughters,' snapped Snaith. 'Completely normal state of affairs.'

'Is it?' asked Ravenscroft in an unbelieving tone, before returning his attention to the younger man. 'Did Miss Fincher ever return to Cirencester?'

'Not as far as I recall.'

'Did your parents ever speak of Miss Fincher?'

'I have no memory of them doing so. All of this has come as rather a shock. I was very surprised to receive Mr Snaith's communication that my cousin had passed away,' said Rupert Fincher in a more confident tone.

'Did you ever visit your cousin here in Colwall?'

'No.'

'Do you know why your cousin left Cirencester?'

'No.'

'Is that all, Ravenscroft?' said Snaith impatiently, tidying up some papers on the table at the side of the chair.

'Did your cousin ever write to you or your family?' asked Ravenscroft. He could tell his interview with the young man was drawing to its end, and he had gained nothing at all from his questioning.

'I think there might have been the occasional letter sent to my parents, but they ceased once my mother and father died.'

'And when was that?'

'My father died fifteen years ago, when I was quite young. My mother passed away ten years ago.'

'I don't suppose you have these letters, Mr Fincher?' asked Crabb.

'No. I am sorry.'

'I think this interview is at an end,' announced Snaith, beginning to rise.

'Where were you last Monday evening?' asked Ravenscroft.

'I, er . . . I was at home in Cirencester,' stuttered Fincher, apparently taken aback by the sudden change in the detective's line of questioning.

'For goodness' sake, Ravenscroft,' groaned Snaith.

'May I ask what your future plans are, Mr Fincher?'

'Gross impertinence! You don't have to answer that question Rupert,' snapped Snaith.

'I was merely enquiring as to how long your client is intending to stay here in Malvern, should we have need to question him further,' said Ravenscroft, determined not to be riled by the solicitor.

'I am not sure,' began the young man, looking earnestly at Snaith.

'Mr Fincher and I have a lot to attend to,' said the solicitor quickly.

'So you will be staying here at the Abbey for the next few days?'

'Yes, I suppose so.'

'Not at Claremont?'

'Claremont?' enquired Fincher.

'Your late cousin's residence in Colwall,' replied Ravenscroft, giving a brief smile.

'Oh yes, Claremont, of course. No, I will be staying here at the Abbey.'

'Thank you, Mr Fincher, I bid you good day. Mr Snaith.'

* * *

'That was a waste of time,' muttered Crabb as the two men walked away from the Abbey Hotel.

'Yes, it was rather disappointing that Rupert Fincher did not provide us with any information concerning his late cousin. It is odd that the young man never met Miss Fincher during her lifetime.'

'Some families are like that. I think it has been five years or more since my wife visited her cousins.'

'Nevertheless, you would have thought that when both his parents had died, leaving Rupert Fincher as an orphan at fifteen years or so, that his cousin might have taken some interest in his well-being — especially as he was her only living relative. And she had a charitable interest in orphans, remember.'

'Yes, it does seem rather strange.'

'Nor was he able to tell us why his cousin had left Cirencester all those years ago. I know that he had not been born then, but you would have thought that his parents would have mentioned the matter at some time.'

'He seemed very uncertain of himself.'

'Yes, and did you notice how he kept looking at Marcus Snaith before he answered our questions, as if he was seeking guidance from the older man.'

'The solicitor certainly seemed over-familiar with his client.'

'Yes, it was almost as though he was shielding him from our questions. And did you observe that when I asked him if he would be staying at Claremont, he did not recognise the name of his cousin's house?'

'That is hardly surprising. He had never received any communication from his cousin.'

'Yes, that could explain the lapse, but something is not quite right here. It is almost as though Rupert Fincher is perhaps not all that he appears to be. This case gets more intriguing as the days go by. Anyway, enough of this. We know where Fincher is staying for the next few days, so he will keep for a while. What I really want to know at the present time is why we have not heard back from the police in Shipston-on-Stour regarding those Moncriefs.'

* * *

'So you are sending poor Tom all the way to Shipston-on-Stour tomorrow,' said Lucy later that evening, as she and her husband sat before a warm fire in their cottage in Ledbury.

'Well, I can't go. I have to attend that séance at the Moncriefs in the early evening, and I might not be back in time,' replied Ravenscroft.

'What exactly did the telegram say?'

'It said that they had never heard of anyone called Moncrief living in the town, although there had been some irregularities concerning a pair of spiritualists called Williamson.'

'What irregularities?'

'I don't know; the telegram did not elaborate.'

'So you think the Moncriefs might really be these Williamsons?'

'They could be. That is why I am sending Tom there tomorrow to find out. If the Moncriefs, or Williamsons, left Shipston under a cloud, I certainly want to know what they got up to during their stay there. I am determined to get to the bottom of this matter.'

'You think that it was the Moncriefs that frightened poor Miss Fincher to death?'

'Something rather unpleasant happened at that last séance. I don't know what it was, but it was enough to make Maud Fincher believe that she was about to die and cause her to write a letter to the Chief Constable. It was a plea for help; it was unfortunate that we received it far too late.'

'I can't help feel sorry for the poor woman, living all alone in that big house with only one maid for company,' said Lucy, laying aside her embroidery.

'It was the life she wanted.'

'That sounds rather harsh. It seems likely that tragic circumstances forced her to leave her hometown all those years ago and seek solitude in Colwall. She may not have had any say in the matter.'

'Perhaps so, but I believe that people make their own futures. I only wish I knew what it was that made her leave. I feel that once we know that, we might be able to work out who caused her death.'

'It may have been all perfectly innocent,' suggested Lucy. 'Tell me more about her cousin, this Rupert Fincher. He sounds quite interesting.'

'I think I have told you all that I can. What else do you want to know?'

'Well, is he handsome, for a start?'

‘Some women might think so.’

‘It cannot have been easy for him to lose both his parents before he had grown up, and hearing nothing from his cousin for all those years.’

‘She did remember him in her will.’

‘So she did the right thing in the end.’

‘I suppose so, but I find it all rather strange.’

‘What do you mean?’

‘Why leave everything you own to a cousin whom you have never seen?’

‘Perhaps she felt guilty.’

‘Guilty?’

‘Guilty — that she had not done anything for him during her lifetime. So what are you going to do about it Samuel?’

‘About what?’

‘Rupert Fincher. I can see that you do not believe the man’s story.’

‘You are right, Lucy. I should pay a visit to Cirencester as soon as possible and make enquiries regarding these Finchers,’ said Ravenscroft, throwing another log on the fire. ‘The only problem is I am due at this séance tomorrow night, and Tom is going to Shipston, so it will have to be the day after tomorrow at the earliest.’

‘That may be too late. Why don’t I go there tomorrow for you, and see what I can find out?’ suggested Lucy enthusiastically.

‘I wouldn’t want to impose on you.’

‘Nonsense! The weather is certain to be good tomorrow, and I would enjoy the opportunity of visiting somewhere new. Cirencester does have a railway station?’

‘It does. When I was looking into that artist after that murder on Hangman Hill, I travelled by rail to Cirencester. There are one or two changes on the way. We could consult Bradshaw.’

‘Then that is settled. I shall go first thing in the morning. If there is anything to learn about these Finchers, I shall be the person to find it out,’ said Lucy with confidence.

‘That would be most helpful, but please do be careful. Look what happened when you went to London on your own.’

‘I am sure that life is a lot safer in a peaceful Cotswold market town than it is the East End of London.’

‘I quite envy you. I wish I was coming with you, but I feel I must go to this wretched séance and see if I can expose these Moncriefs for the charlatans that they are.’

‘Then it is you who needs to be careful,’ said Lucy.

CHAPTER SEVEN

WEDNESDAY

The following morning, Ravenscroft, having bid farewell to both Lucy and Crabb as they went on their respective journeys, made his way down the Homend towards Ledbury Police Station.

Now that he was alone with his thoughts, he found himself going over the events of the previous few days, and he began to consider the possibility that there was probably no case to answer at all. Maud Fincher had died of natural causes. Her heart had given out due to anxiety and worry. The fact that the only window in her bedroom had not been secured might have been no more than a mere coincidence. Perhaps the Moncriefs were innocent of any crime, merely being well-meaning types whose only desire was to ease the suffering experienced by the bereaved. Perhaps Rupert Fincher was who he said he was — a young man who had lost both his parents when young, and who had been disregarded by his only living relative. He told himself that perhaps he was trying to make something from nothing; one last case that needed solving, whatever the cost, when really there was nothing to investigate at all.

That all seemed perfectly understandable — and yet all his years of experience now told him that something was not quite right. Someone had caused Maud Fincher to fear for her life. Someone had then caused her death. There was now a legacy, and Rupert Fincher appeared to be the only benefactor. Had he caused his cousin's death? After all, he could have no kind feelings for an old woman who had ignored him for all those years. Then there was Maud Fincher's secret. Why had she left Cirencester all those years ago? Why had she become estranged from her own parents? Why had she never sought out her only living relative?

And what about the Moncriefs? Since they had arrived in the area, some six months ago, they had created a circle of those people who had lost loved ones. Were they now preying on these vulnerable people, perhaps extracting money from them? It sounded rather like they were attempting to coerce Mr Fanshawe into building them a spiritualist church in Malvern Link. Was their real name Williamson, and if so, had they been forced to leave Shipston-on-Stour before the law had caught up with them? Ravenscroft knew that he would not be able answer many of these questions until Crabb and Lucy had returned later that evening. Until then he would try to distract his thoughts away from the case, however frustrating that might be.

Ravenscroft increased his pace as he thought, and was going at speed as he turned the corner into the marketplace. This was unfortunate, as he collided with someone coming the other way.

'I am so terribly sorry,' said Ravenscroft, recovering his balance and looking down at the tweed-suited man who lay at his feet. 'Here let me help you up.'

'You should look where you are going!' snapped the man, refusing Ravenscroft's extended hand as he struggled to his feet.

'I was deep in thought. The fault was entirely mine. I hope you are not hurt ?'

'No, I'm fine,' said the man dusting himself down, apparently placated by Ravenscroft's apology.

'That is good. My apologies once again.' said Ravenscroft.

'Perhaps the fault was mine.'

'No, I can assure you that the fault was entirely my own,' said Ravenscroft raising his hat.

'I wonder if you can tell me where the police station is in this town?'

'Dear me, I hope you are not going to make a complaint.'

'No, not at all,' replied the other, appreciating Ravenscroft's joke.

'I am going there myself, if you would care to accompany me.'

'Thank you, sir.'

'You are a stranger to these parts?' asked Ravenscroft as the two men moved away from the marketplace.

'Yes, first time in Ledbury. It seems a most attractive town.'

'It is.'

'It appears to be a great improvement on Evesham.'

'I thought Evesham was quite pleasant,' said Ravenscroft. 'Ah, here we are; after you.'

The two men stepped into the outer room of the police station.

'Now, how can I help you?' said Ravenscroft.

'Oh, I see. You work here?' replied the other, somewhat taken aback.

'Indeed I do. How can I be of assistance?'

'Yes, my name is Alphonse Bracket.'

'That is quite an unusual name,' remarked Ravenscroft.

'Bracket, you mean?'

'Alphonse.'

'Oh, my parents had ideas of French grandeur when I was born. You must be Samuel Ravenscroft?'

'Yes, but how do you know my name?' asked the detective.

'I take it you have not yet received a communication from the Chief Constable?'

'No,' said Ravenscroft, finding himself suddenly adopting a defensive manner.

'Oh, this is all rather embarrassing.' The newcomer shuffled his feet.

'Let me see,' said Ravenscroft searching below the counter. 'Ah yes, here we are. The letter must have arrived earlier this morning.'

'It seems that I am to be your replacement. I am Detective Inspector Bracket, newly promoted.'

'Where were you posted before?' asked Ravenscroft, opening the letter and studying its contents.

'I was sergeant at Evesham for the past five years.'

'Oh yes, you said. You appear to be rather young to be promoted,' muttered Ravenscroft, laying the letter down on the counter.

'Yes, I suppose they were running out of people. People to promote, that is,' replied Bracket uneasily.

'It says in the letter that you are to take over next Monday.'

'Yes, I gather so.'

'I was under the impression that I was not due to take my retirement until the end of the month,' said Ravenscroft, feeling increasingly annoyed.

'I am afraid I don't know anything about that. They just said report for duty in Ledbury next Monday. I am sorry if this has come as a shock,' said Bracket, looking down at the floor.

'So why are you here today?' asked Ravenscroft.

'I had the day off, so I thought I would come and introduce myself and have a look around.'

'Have a look around?' retorted Ravenscroft.

'Yes. I realise now that this was not a particularly good idea.'

'It was not,' snapped Ravenscroft.

'Yes, I can see that. I will go now. I am glad I have met you. I will see you next Monday.'

Ravenscroft said nothing.

'Yes, I will see you next week.' Crestfallen, Bracket stepped out of the door and into the street.

Ravenscroft looked sternly out of the window.

'Damn! How dare they!' he exclaimed, bringing his first down hard on to the counter. 'Damn them!'

* * *

Ravenscroft strode across Link Common towards the Moncriefs' house later that day. After his annoyance at the morning's news, he was now even more determined to proceed with the investigation into Maud Fincher's death as soon as possible. He realised he had only a few days left before he would be compelled to relinquish his duties, and he had no desire to pass over an unfinished case to his successor. If the Moncriefs were behind Maud Fincher's demise then he would be able to charge them, and that would be a satisfactory end to the matter. He would then be able to step down with dignity and a sense of achievement. He wanted to avoid any loose ends, but until Crabb and Lucy returned he had very little to go on.

Professor Moncrief opened the front door before Ravenscroft could even bring his hand down on the woodwork. 'Ah, Inspector Ravenscroft, please do come in. The others are all waiting for us.'

Ravenscroft stepped into the hallway, took off his coat and hat, laid them on the hall table, and followed his host down the corridor and into the drawing room.

'Inspector Ravenscroft,' announced Moncrief.

'So nice to see you again,' said Janet Moncrief, coming forwards to greet the detective. She linked his arm in hers.

'It was kind of you to invite me,' replied Ravenscroft, startled by the sudden intimacy.

'I think you know everyone here,' said Moncrief indicating the group seated at the large round table. 'Miss Jayward, Mrs Tinniswood, Colonel Mortimer and Mr Fanshawe.'

'Yes, indeed. Good evening to you all,' replied Ravenscroft observing that Mr Fanshawe was standing aloof at the other end of the room.

'Who is that, dear?' whispered Mrs Tinniswood, addressing her companion.

'That nice inspector. You remember, he visited us the other day,' replied Miss Jayward.

'Oh yes, I remember.'

'Can I offer you some refreshment, Inspector?' asked Moncrief.

'No, thank you.'

'I am so pleased that you could all come this evening to our little gathering,' said Janet Moncrief. 'Let us hope the spirits are in good form this evening.'

'What did she say?' asked Miss Tinniswood.

'Janet said that she thought things would go well tonight,' replied her companion.

'Oh, yes.'

'Then perhaps we should begin. Now if you sit there, Inspector. Janet, if you will sit in your usual place. I will just light the candle and then draw the curtains. Would you care to join us, Mr Fanshawe?'

Fanshawe said nothing as he walked over and took his seat. Moncrief lit a solitary candle in the centre of the table, before plunging the room into near darkness as he pulled the heavy curtains across the windows.

Ravenscroft adjusted his spectacles and looked around the table — on either side of him were Janet Moncrief and Miss Jayward, with Fanshawe and Mortimer next to them, then Miss Tinniswood, and finally Moncrief himself who sat at the head of the circle opposite his wife.

'Let us all join hands in the usual manner,' instructed Moncrief.

Ravenscroft felt the cold grip of Janet Moncrief's hand as she reached out and gave him a brief smile of encouragement.

'Let us close our eyes, brothers and sisters,' continued Moncrief.

Ravenscroft closed his eyes for a few seconds and listened to the sounds of heavy breathing and the ticking of a distant clock and wondered if it had been the wise thing to do to have come to the séance. Opening his eyes, he found Fanshawe's sullen gaze was on him. The flame from the solitary candle appeared to flicker backwards and forwards, casting fleeting shadows on the faces of the other members.

Another minute or so passed. Janet Moncrief's breathing became heavier and deeper. Ravenscroft grew uneasy. He had not expected such prolonged inactivity.

Suddenly, her grip tightened on his hand. Janet Moncrief let out a low, guttural sound.

'Is that you, Silas?' asked Professor Moncrief.

Ravenscroft's hand shook as Janet Moncrief issued a louder moaning noise.

'Silas, is that you?' repeated Moncrief. 'Speak to us, if you will.'

'It is I, Silas Crabbit,' said a strange masculine voice that seemed to Ravenscroft to be coming out of the mouth of his hostess.

Mrs Tinniswood gave a slight cry of excitement, as Fanshawe leaned forwards in anticipation.

'Will you speak with us, Silas?' asked Moncrief.

'It is I, Silas Crabbit. There is someone I wish to speak with,' continued the guttural voice.

'Who is it, Silas? Who do you wish to speak with?' continued Moncrief staring intently at his wife.

'It is Amy,' said a new, distant female voice.

'Amy?' cried out Miss Jayward.

'It is Amy,' repeated the voice.

'Amy. Is it you?' asked Miss Jayward.

'Amy Jayward.'

There followed a long pause, during which Ravenscroft wondered if that was an end to the proceedings.

'Silas, will you ask Amy to say a few words to her dear sister?' asked Moncrief.

'Emily. Emily,' repeated the sing-song voice.

Ravenscroft looked round at the various faces and saw that they were all looking intently in Janet Moncrief's direction.

'Amy, it is me, Emily. Are you well?' asked Miss Jayward, leaning forwards. 'Tell me that you are well.'

'Amy says that she is in good health and that she is very happy in her new life,' interjected the masculine voice.

'Oh, I am so glad. May I speak with her again?'

'Amy has to go now, but she says she will speak with you again next time.'

'Thank God for dear Amy. She has spoken to us!' exclaimed Miss Jayward happily.

'Who was that?' asked a puzzled Mrs Tinniswood.

'It was Amy, my late sister.'

'How exciting.'

'There is someone else who has asked me to pass on a message,' continued Crabbit.

'Who? Who?' asked Moncrief.

'I have a message for the Colonel.'

'Daphne?' called out Mortimer, startled and eager.

'There is a message for the Colonel.'

'Yes, yes. You have a message from Daphne?' asked Mortimer.

'I have a message from Daphne. She says that you have been anxious of late, that you have been worrying.'

'Yes, yes.'

'Daphne says that you are not to worry. Although things are hard at present, they will become easier with the passing of time. In the meantime you are to be guided by others, who have your best interests at heart. You must give way to wiser counsel.'

'Yes, yes,' repeated Mortimer anxiously.

'Daphne says you are to be at peace now.'

'Yes.' Relieved, Mortimer slumped back in his chair.

As the silence resumed, Ravenscroft became both more uneasy and more sceptical regarding what he had just witnessed. The whole thing, with Janet Moncrief speaking in different voices, had clearly gripped the circle of friends, but to him it had all seemed to confirm his suspicions that the Moncriefs were taking advantage of the bereaved.

'There is someone new tonight,' announced the Silas Crabbit voice. 'There is someone here who is a doubter.'

'Yes, Silas, we have a new member joining us tonight,' answered Moncrief excitedly.

'Is his name Ravenscroft?'

The detective said nothing as Moncrief answered the question.

'There is someone here who wants to pass on a message to Ravenscroft,' continued Crabbit. 'Let me speak with him.'

'Inspector, if you would be so kind,' urged Moncrief.

'Yes, I am Ravenscroft,' replied the hesitant detective, unsure of what to say and wondering where all this was leading.

'I have a message for Ravenscroft,' said Crabbit. 'You have lost someone who was very close to you.'

Ravenscroft became conscious of the perspiration on his forehead. The grip on his hand tightened again.

'There is someone who once loved you very much. A sibling, perhaps? I see the letter A.'

'Anne,' blurted out Ravenscroft. 'She was my sister.'

'Anne says she is being well cared for in the afterlife. She has always looked over you and kept you safe.'

Ravenscroft's heart was racing. The grip on his hand had intensified almost to the point of pain.

'Anne senses that you are worried about things, and she tells you that you do not need to fear for the future. All will be well. She will continue to look after you, always.'

Ravenscroft wanted to cry out, but he found that the unexpectedness and suddenness of the occasion had rendered him speechless.

'Anne says that you are due to face an unknown danger and that everything will be at risk.'

'What do you mean?' asked Ravenscroft.

'It is time to go now. Anne is taking her leave, but she will return to safeguard you. Anne Ravenscroft, Anne Ravenscroft,' repeated the voice, as it seemed to drift upwards to the ceiling together with the smoke from the solitary candle.

'Balderdash!' exclaimed Fanshawe.

A gust of wind seemed to grip the flickering flame before it extinguished itself in one sudden moment.

The tight grip on Ravenscroft's hand was relinquished, as an unexpected feeling of exhaustion threatened to overwhelm him. He became conscious of someone moving in the darkened room as he slumped back in his chair.

'I will just open the curtains,' said a familiar voice.

Ravenscroft blinked as daylight filled the room. Janet Moncrief appeared to be asleep in her chair. Miss Jayward and Miss Tinniswood were whispering together. He noticed that Colonel Mortimer's face was ashen, while Fanshawe looked up at the ceiling as he drummed his fingers on the table.

Ravenscroft rose quickly from his chair, anxious to rid himself of the claustrophobic room and its inhabitants as soon as possible. 'If you will excuse me, I have another appointment to keep.'

'Yes of course, my dear fellow,' said Moncrief.

Ravenscroft walked quickly out of the room and into the hallway. Moncrief followed him out.

'I hope the experience has been not been too unnerving for you,' said Moncrief as Ravenscroft reached out for his hat and coat. 'The first time is always rather unsettling, but that will quickly pass. You are most welcome to attend our next gathering.'

'Good night, Professor Moncrief.' Shaken and profoundly disturbed, Ravenscroft strode away from the house.

* * *

'Excuse me, I wonder if you could tell me the way to the street that leads up to the entrance to Cirencester Park?' asked Lucy, just after she had alighted from the train.

'Well, my dear, so you is a stranger to the town?' answered the old woman, drawing her shawl tightly around her shoulders.

'Yes indeed,' replied Lucy. 'I am looking for Mr Fincher's residence. I was told he lived in a house near the Park.'

'I has never heard of anyone called Fincher,' grinned the old woman displaying a set of blackened crooked teeth.

'Oh, dear.'

'You say you wants the street near the Park?'

'Yes. Indeed.'

'That will be Cecily Hill. If you follows that road round,' said the old woman pointing. 'And you then enters Park Street, continue along there and you will find the road you want on your left.'

'Thank you, I am much obliged.'

'Never heard of the Finchers,' called out the old woman as Lucy set off at a brisk pace.

Her journey to Cirencester that morning had been uneventful. She resolved that once she had found the home of Rupert Fincher, she would then explore what appeared to be an inviting prospect, before her return to Ledbury later in the day.

A few minutes later Lucy turned into a wide street, where a collection of fine two- and three-storey Georgian houses, built of honey-coloured brick and stone, and displaying impressive painted front doors, stood grandly on either side. The road itself followed a slight incline upwards, leading to what she supposed was the entrance to Cirencester Park.

Walking up to the first building on her left, she rang the bell-pull.

'Good day, miss,' said a young woman dressed in a servant's attire.

'Good morning. I am sorry to disturb you, but I am given to understand that this might be the house of Mr Rupert Fincher,' said Lucy somewhat hesitantly.

'You must be mistaken, miss. Mrs Gladstone lives here.'

'Then I must have the wrong house. Perhaps you would be kind enough, then, to inform me where Mr Fincher lives.'

'Sorry, miss, I have heard of no one of that name living in this street.'

'Oh dear,' said a crestfallen Lucy.

'But I have only been here for little over a year.'

'Then perhaps I will ask elsewhere.'

Reasoning that she was unlikely to find the Fincher home in the near vicinity if the maid had not heard of the family, Lucy decided to walk further up the road. As she was about to knock on the door of one of the houses, it was suddenly flung open and a bald man clutching a pile of books under his arm rushed quickly past her.

'Can you tell me if Mr Fincher lives here?' called out Lucy.

'Never heard of any Finchers,' shouted out the man as he strode quickly down the road. 'Sorry, can't wait! Late for choir practice.'

Undaunted, Lucy crossed the road and rang the bell of one of the houses.

'Yes, what do you want?' snapped a stout, middle-aged woman, opening the door and quickly eyeing the new arrival.

'I am sorry to disturb you,' began Lucy.

'You have. Come to the point.'

'I was looking for the residence of Mr Rupert Fincher. I believe he resides somewhere in Cecily Hill.'

'I have never heard of anyone called Fincher. Now good day to you,' replied the woman, abruptly slamming the door in Lucy's face.

During the next few minutes, Lucy knocked on a further three doors, but not one of their occupants knew the Fincher family.

Lucy sighed and made her way down the street. Perhaps the information that she had received from her husband had been incorrect? Perhaps Rupert Fincher had lied when he had said he had lived in Cirencester? It looked as though she would have to return home, her mission unfulfilled.

'Good morning to you, miss. You looks all-about to me.'

Lucy turned round to see a grey-haired man smoking a wooden pipe, leaning against a stone wall.

'All-about?'

'Ye be all upside down, confused, like.'

'Yes, I am afraid I am,' replied Lucy.

'You is a stranger to Cirencester?'

'Yes indeed.'

'Then maybes I can help ye. Giles Strongbow, aged gravedigger and candlemaker of this parish at your service, miss.'

'Well, Mr Strongbow, I do believe that you may be of assistance to me. I was informed that Mr Rupert Fincher lived in this street.'

'Fincher, you says?' The old man scratched his head and rolled his eyes up at the sky. 'Finchers has never lived up this street, and I has lived in the town for near seventy years.'

'Oh, dear,' sighed Lucy.

'But there is some Finchers in Cirencester. They be not far away from here.'

'Would it be possible for you to take me there? I will pay you for your time and trouble,' said Lucy eagerly.

'No trouble, if you would care to come with me.'

Lucy followed the old man along two narrow streets where the smaller stone-built houses seemed to crowd in one upon another.

'That's where the Finchers lived,' said Strongbow, coming to a halt on the corner of a street.

Lucy looked across at the sorry-looking house with its closed shutters, and peeling paint on its window frames and front door.

'That's where old Jasper and his wife Margaret once lived. I remember old Jasper. I once threw a stone at one of his windows, when I was a boy, and broke it. He did not half give me a telling off, I can tell you,' chuckled the old man.

'The house looks rather neglected,' observed Lucy.

'It has been empty for these past few years.'

'That is rather sad.'

'Expect it be quite damp inside, I be bound, as it has been empty for so long.'

'I believe that they had a daughter.'

'Yes, there was a girl.'

'Maud Fincher,' offered Lucy.

'Maud Fincher, you says? That could be her.'

'Do you remember Mr Rupert Fincher?'

'Oh yes, that be old Jasper's nephew, if I am not mistaken. Rupert Fincher. That will be him, to be sure.'

'Yes, that is the one. Can you tell me where Mr Fincher lives now?' asked Lucy hopefully.

'Oh, I don't know as I can help you there.'

'But why ever not?'

'You sure you wants to know?' Strongbow stared intently into Lucy's face.

'Yes, yes, please take me to where I might find Mr Fincher,' pleaded Lucy, determined that she was not going to give up on her search now that she had come so far.

'Then you best come with me.'

Lucy followed Strongbow down an even narrower street until they reached a worn, rusty creaking gate.

'This way,' instructed the old man pushing open the gate.

Lucy hesitantly entered the garden, wondering why the old man had taken her to this strange and forlorn place.

'You wants to know where Rupert Fincher is?' asked Giles Strongbow, after they had walked on a few yards.

'Yes, of course,' answered Lucy eagerly.

'That's where he is,' said Strongbow, pointing to one of the headstones. 'Rupert Fincher, late of this parish — he's been dead these past eight years!'

CHAPTER EIGHT

'Dead, you say!' exclaimed Ravenscroft.

It was later that night, and husband and wife had just been reunited in their cottage in Ledbury.

'I saw Rupert Fincher's gravestone. It said that he had died eight years ago. He was only twenty-six at the time of his death.'

'This changes everything. Did your informant tell you how Fincher had died?' asked Ravenscroft leading the way into the living room.

'He could not recall the exact cause of death, although apparently there had been a lot of illness in the town that year. It seems a very young age to be taken.'

'So the Rupert Fincher who attended the funeral is clearly an imposter. Snaith said he had contacted him in Cirencester. He is clearly lying. I knew there was something not quite right about that man.' Ravenscroft poured out some whisky from the decanter, and handed one of the tumblers to Lucy.

'Perhaps the imposter intercepted the telegram and decided to impersonate the real Rupert Fincher,' suggested Lucy.

'No, it is more than likely that Snaith read about Maud Fincher's death in the newspaper and saw an opportunity to take possession of her estate. He must have put someone up to impersonate the dead Rupert Fincher. First thing tomorrow morning, Tom and I will go over to Malvern and arrest the pair of them.'

'Do you think they could have killed Maud Fincher?'

'I would not put that past them,' said Ravenscroft, throwing another log on the fire. 'I am sorry to have put you through that hunt. It could not have been easy for you, my dear.'

'Oh, I did not mind at all. At one time I thought I would never find the Fincher house. It was my good fortune that I came across the old gravedigger, who showed me the house and was able to take me to where Rupert Fincher was buried.'

'And you say the Fincher house was all closed up?'

'Yes, it looked as though it had not been lived in for many years. It was sadly neglected.'

'That is interesting.'

'The gravedigger, Mr Strongbow, also informed me that Rupert Fincher was the last of his line. There are no Finchers left in Cirencester now.'

'So Maud Fincher really was alone in the world. I wonder if her cousin was already dead by this time she made her will?' wondered Ravenscroft.

'Now tell me all about your séance,' asked Lucy.

'There is not much to relate really. Miss Jayward, Mr Fanshawe, Mrs Tinniswood and Colonel Mortimer were all present, and the Moncriefs, of course. They drew the curtains so that the only light came from a solitary candle. We all sat round a large table and held hands. There was lots of heavy breathing, and then Janet Moncrief began to speak in all these strange voices.' Ravenscroft paused to sip his drink.

Lucy detected the slight wavering in her husband's voice and placed her hand on his arm. 'I can see that the séance has upset you.'

'No not really. Janet Moncrief began speaking in the Crabbit voice. She, or he, first spoke to one or two of the others, and then suddenly she said she had spoken to my late sister.'

'Anne, you mean?'

'Yes. She said Anne was in a good place and was always looking out for me. It unsettled me, I can tell you, although I did not believe a word of it. Then Fanshawe shouted out loud, and the whole thing came to an abrupt end.'

'How awful,' sympathised Lucy.

'I left as soon as I could.' Ravenscroft downed the rest of his glass in one swallow.

'Do you think the Moncriefs are genuine, or not?'

'To tell you the truth, I do not know what they are up to. It was all very theatrical, the tight holding of hands, the darkened room, the strange sounds, the voices. I can see how easily it would be for vulnerable people to be taken in by such goings-on.'

'I think they are clearly not to be trusted,' said Lucy.

'We will know more when Tom returns from Shipston, although it is rather late, and I do not expect him until tomorrow. That is not all that has happened today. I met my successor.'

'You mean the man who is going to take over from you?'

'Yes, he turned up this morning. Apparently the Chief Constable has decided that I am to retire next Monday.'

'But they cannot do that. They said you would not be leaving until the end of the month.'

'The Chief Constable's word is not to be trusted. I would have thought that after all these years of loyal service they would have treated me with some dignity and respect,' grumbled Ravenscroft.

'Oh Samuel, I am so sorry.'

'There you have it. I just wanted to get to the bottom of this wretched case before I retired. I don't like loose ends. I want to bring whoever is responsible for Maud Fincher's death to justice. You understand that?'

'Of course. What is your successor like?'

'He is a young, jumped-up man in a loud checked suit, who goes by the name of Alphonse Bracket.'

'Alphonse Bracket!' said Lucy, trying to suppress a laugh. 'Alphonse Bracket. I cannot believe that anyone can be called Alphonse Bracket.'

'Well, it appears to be his name. We cannot help what our parents decide to call us. We have no say in the matter.'

'But you would have thought he would have changed his name to something else.'

'You mean like Jones, or Smith, or something plain like that. Perhaps he rather likes his name.'

'How old is he?'

'About thirty, I would say. He has just been promoted from Sergeant in Evesham. At that age I was still a constable in Whitechapel. Nowadays they seem to promote policemen before they can walk,' moaned Ravenscroft. 'I don't know how poor Tom is going to get on with him.'

'Excuse me, sir,' said the maid suddenly entering the room. 'It is Constable Crabb. He says sorry for the late hour, but he has some news for you.'

'Sergeant Crabb,' corrected Ravenscroft. 'Yes, show him in without delay. Hello, Tom, it is good to see you.'

'Good evening, sir,' said Crabb. 'And Mrs Ravenscroft. I am sorry to disturb you at such a late hour.'

'It is no matter, dear fellow. Take a seat,' said Ravenscroft enthusiastically.

'Tom, it is good to see you. Samuel why don't you give the poor man a drink?' said Lucy.'

'Yes of course,' said Ravenscroft. 'We were just talking about you. How did you get on in Shipston-on-Stour?'

'Well, I went first to the police station,' said Crabb accepting the drink, 'and they could tell me practically nothing at all except they had heard quite a lot of bad gossip in the town concerning the Williamsons before they left, but there was nothing of a criminal nature.'

'Go on,' urged Ravenscroft.

'So I decided to ask around. I went round several businesses, shopkeepers and such like, and they all said the couple had a bad reputation in the town — not paying their store tab, that sort of thing. They had held various public meetings, which some people had attended, some of whom had gone on to have private sessions in the Williamsons' rented house. From the descriptions that they gave me, I think we can safely say that these Williamsons are our Moncriefs.'

'Splendid!' said Ravenscroft.

'However I could find no evidence of money changing hands. If any of the people I spoke to gave them donations, they didn't own up to the fact.'

'That is understandable.'

'Then I had a word with the local vicar, a man by the name of Goodwin. He was very much against the Williamsons, saying that they had preyed on his congregation, even taking people away from his church. I think he was instrumental in driving the Williamsons away from the town.'

'Well done, Tom. So the Moncriefs did arrive here from Shipston, where they previously called themselves Williamson. The pattern seems the same, holding a public meeting, then inviting the more susceptible into their home for séances, but you say you could not discover any financial wrongdoing on their part?'

'That would appear so.'

'This is all rather frustrating. It would have been more valuable to us had we found any former impropriety,' said Ravenscroft.

'So what is your news, sir?' asked Crabb.

'I can tell you that both Mrs Ravenscroft and I have had a very productive day, and that tomorrow morning you and I will be in a position to make an arrest.'

CHAPTER NINE

THURSDAY

The following morning Ravenscroft and Crabb once again stood outside the Abbey Hotel in the centre of Great Malvern.

'It will be interesting to see what this young man has to say for himself,' said Ravenscroft.

'You think he could be responsible for causing Maud Fincher's death?' asked Crabb.

'It seems most likely, and I believe that Snaith put him up to impersonating the dead woman's cousin.'

'I never did like that man. There was something you could not trust about him.'

'Snaith can wait,' replied Ravenscroft, striding up the steps of the hotel, and then briskly in through the large doors.

'Good morning, gentlemen. How can I be of assistance?' said the tall clerk standing behind the reception counter. 'We have a number of comfortable rooms available at the present time at very favourable prices, and some with excellent views of the surrounding area.'

'No thank you, we do not intend staying. We would like to see one of your guests, Mr Rupert Fincher. Is he in the Breakfast Room?' asked Ravenscroft, anxious to push forward with the matter as soon as possible.

'I do not believe so,' replied the man.

'I hope that Mr Fincher has not left the hotel?'

'No. He is still with us.'

'Have you seen him this morning?'

'No, sir.'

'Then he must still be in his room.'

'I presume so. Would you like me to send a message up to his room?'

'No, we will make our own way there, if you would be kind enough to tell us the number.'

'I am afraid I cannot do that, sir. It would be quite unethical, very much against the rules of the hotel,' protested the clerk, in what Ravenscroft detected to be in a superior tone of voice.

'I am Detective Inspector Ravenscroft, and this is my colleague Sergeant Crabb. It is most important that I speak with Mr Fincher right now. Your name is?'

'Collins. I am the Senior Receptionist at the hotel.'

'Well, Mr Collins, I am sure you would not want to obstruct us in the carrying out of our duties,' emphasised Ravenscroft.

'As I said, Inspector, I can send a message up to the young gentleman.'

'We have reason to believe that Mr Fincher is not who he declares himself to be —that he is impersonating a dead man.'

'Oh dear,' exclaimed the clerk.

'I fear that if we send a message to his room, the gentleman might have cause to affect his escape,' emphasised Ravenscroft.

'Perhaps it might be better if I accompanied you to Mr Fincher's room,' whispered the clerk. 'I would appreciate your discretion in this matter, Inspector. I am sure we would not want the other guests to be alarmed.'

'Indeed not,' said Ravenscroft, giving a brief smile.

Collins took down a large key from the rack behind him. 'If you would care to follow me.'

The two detectives followed the receptionist along a long corridor, and up a flight of creaking wooden stairs.

'This is Mr Fincher's room,' announced Collins, pausing outside one of the rooms.

'Would you be kind enough to open the door,' asked Ravenscroft.

'I think it might be more expeditious if I knocked first.'

'Very well, Mr Collins.'

The clerk rapped gently on the door.

The three men looked at one another.

'Perhaps a little harder,' said Collins, repeating his action.

'I think we should unlock the door,' suggested Ravenscroft, after some moments had elapsed.

The receptionist inserted the key in the lock, and slowly opened the door.

Ravenscroft and Crabb strode into the room.

'It seems that Mr Fincher is not here,' said Collins, casting his eyes around the room.

'His bed does not appear to have been slept in,' remarked Crabb.

'Could the maid have made up the bed this morning?' enquired Ravenscroft.

'I believe not. We usually make up the beds after breakfast,' replied Collins.

'Well, it certainly seems that Mr Fincher did not sleep here last night. Check whether he has left his luggage behind, Tom.'

'This is all most unusual,' remarked the receptionist.

'Did you see Mr Fincher go up to his room last night?' asked Ravenscroft.

'Yes, he went up shortly after dinner.'

'What time would that have been?'

'Just after eight o'clock.'

'Did you see him come down the stairs again?' asked Ravenscroft.

'No, I don't believe so. I manned the desk until morning and didn't see anyone.'

'So he could have left the hotel after that time without you seeing him depart?'

'That is possible.'

'There are other exits from the hotel?' continued Ravenscroft.

'Yes, there is a side exit, which leads down towards the park.'

'So he could have left that way, without anyone seeing him.'

'That could be what happened.'

'This is his luggage,' said Crabb, retrieving a battered leather case from inside the wardrobe and placing it on the bed.

Ravenscroft inspected it. 'This case has seen better days.' He flipped it open.

'Oh, I really must protest,' murmured the clerk.

'Two or three shirts,' went on Ravenscroft, 'some underwear, nothing to make him stand out from anyone else, although this looks interesting — an old hip flask, empty, but engraved on the back, "Adam Pendleton. 1890."'

'That must be his real name,' suggested Crabb.

'I think you are correct. Obviously this was given to our man three years ago, perhaps to mark his twenty-first birthday or something like that. It is a pity there is nothing else to tell us where he came from.'

As Ravenscroft searched the case, Crabb had been looking underneath the bed and opening the drawers of the other furniture in the room, much to the clerk's dismay.

'There is nothing further here,' he announced. 'He has left his brush and comb set on the side table over there.'

Ravenscroft turned back to the unhappy clerk. 'Do you recall if Mr Fincher, as he called himself, received any visitors yesterday?'

'None I can remember. Oh yes, Mr Snaith the solicitor was here about three thirty in the afternoon.'

'How long was he here for?'

'About fifteen minutes. They talked together in the lounge, then Mr Snaith left rather hurriedly.'

'That is interesting. How was Mr Snaith when he left?' asked Ravenscroft. 'Was he angry, for instance? You say he left rather quickly.'

'Oh yes, now you mention it. He did seem a trifle annoyed.'

'But you don't know what the cause of that annoyance was?'

'No, as I said the gentlemen had been conversing together in the lounge. It is not the custom of this hotel to pry into its guests' conversations,' replied Collins, his tone somewhat pointed.

'Of course not. Did Mr Fincher, or the man posing as him, receive any other visitors yesterday?'

'No. I don't think he did. But he did receive a letter later that afternoon.'

'Do you happen to know where this letter came from?'

'No. There was no address on the outside, although I did observe that it had been posted earlier that day in Malvern.'

'Did the letter arrive before or after Mr Snaith visited Mr Fincher?'

'It was after. It was about half an hour before dinner, if I recall correctly.'

'And can you tell me what happened to that letter?'

'I sent it straight up to Mr Fincher's room. That was the last I saw of it.'

'There is no sign of the letter lying about anywhere,' said Crabb. 'He must have taken it out with him.'

As they took their leave of the fretful clerk and returned to their horse and trap, Ravenscroft ran through what they had discovered.

'So, Fincher receives a visit from Snaith yesterday afternoon. They talk for some minutes. Snaith leaves in an angry mood. An hour or so later Fincher receives a letter. He dines alone, and then sometime after eight o'clock in the evening he leaves the hotel, probably by a side entrance, and fails to return.'

'The letter must have been summoning him to a meeting,' suggested Crabb.

'Yes, but he obviously intended returning to the Abbey Hotel to sleep that evening, as he left all his personal effects here. I wonder who his correspondent was?'

'It could be someone who had found out his deception?'

'Possibly. It is a pity we don't have the letter,' said Ravenscroft. 'The fact that he did not return to his room last night when he fully intended to is most disturbing. I wonder if anything has happened to this young man? Who the devil was he meeting last night? What was so important to him that it made him leave the hotel after dinner? If only he had been here this morning, we might have concluded this case by now.'

'There is still Mr Snaith, sir.'

'Yes, he must have known that this Adam Pendleton was not Rupert Fincher. He holds all the answers. Time we visited the gentleman.'

* * *

'I had almost forgotten how bad these steps were,' said Ravenscroft, breathing heavily as he and Crabb made their way up the two flights to the solicitor's office.

'I don't know why people choose to work in such inaccessible places,' gasped Crabb.

'Cheapness. Ah, here we are at last. I hope our visit will be worth it,' said Ravenscroft pausing to steady his breathing, before knocking on the door.

Without waiting to receive an answer, he pushed open the door and the two detectives stepped quickly into the room.

'Ah it is Inspector Ravenscroft, is it not?' said the old clerk, looking up from his ledger.

'Is Mr Snaith here?' demanded Ravenscroft.

'Well yes, but Mr Snaith is very busy. He cannot be disturbed.'

'Mr Snaith is always busy. We will see him now,' replied Ravenscroft, walking briskly past the clerk.

'I must really protest,' spluttered the clerk rising from his stool, an anxious look on his face as Ravenscroft and Crabb disappeared from view down the corridor.

'Mr Snaith,' said Ravenscroft, abruptly throwing open the door to Snaith's office.

'What the devil?' protested the solicitor, looking up from some papers he was reading on his desk.

'I am so sorry, Mr Snaith. The Inspector was most insistent that he see you,' said the flustered clerk from behind them.

'You and I need to talk, Snaith,' said Ravenscroft in an urgent tone of voice, as he stared across the table at the solicitor.

'That is alright, Gibbons, you can leave us now. I will deal with this,' said Snaith.

'Very well,' said the clerk, closing the door behind him as he left the room.

'May I know the reason for this outrage, Inspector?' demanded Snaith.

'We know that you put Adam Pendleton up to impersonating Rupert Fincher,' declared Ravenscroft coming straight to the point.

'Who is this Pendleton?'

'The man you told to claim he was Rupert Fincher.'

'I don't know what you are talking about.'

'We have visited the town of Cirencester. It might interest you to know that Rupert Fincher died eight years ago.'

'Who says so?'

'His gravestone and his empty house say so,' said Ravenscroft, trying not to become angered by the solicitor's intransigence and lofty manner.

'If what you say is true, and I must emphasise, most strongly, the word "if,"' replied Snaith, taking an infuriatingly superior tone, 'I can assure you that I have been acting in a most proper and ethical manner. When I learned of Miss Fincher's death, I retrieved her will from our archives, which you saw in this office Ravenscroft, and which stated quite clearly that her sole heir was her cousin Rupert Fincher. I sent telegrams to Cirencester to track down the said gentleman. When I received a reply from Mr Fincher, I informed him of his inheritance, and as you saw he came over here for his cousin's funeral.'

'That is all nonsense, as you well know, Snaith,' retorted the detective.

'I have no reason to suppose that the man is not genuine.'

'You put this imposter Adam Pendleton up to impersonating a dead man so that you and he could share the old woman's estate,' said Ravenscroft, banging his fist hard on the desk.

'Have a care what you say next, have a care, or you will shortly find yourself in a court of law, where you will answer for these slanderous insults.'

'And I have no doubt you would employ the best man you could to represent you. Sefton Rawlinson comes to mind,' retorted Ravenscroft.

'Who the devil is this Sefton Rawlinson? Have you gone mad Ravenscroft? I have told you I have acted in the best of faith in this matter. I believe the man to be Rupert Fincher, and that is all there is to it. You will have the deuce to prove otherwise.'

'If, as you claim, you believed this man Pendleton to be Rupert Fincher, why did you not see fit to check his identity?' asked Ravenscroft.

'I had fully intended to do so. In fact Mr Fincher had promised me that he would produce documentary evidence as to his identity within the next few days. I had no cause to doubt him. You have clearly been misinformed as to this man's identity. I wish you good day Ravenscroft,' replied Snaith dismissively.

'What were you doing at the Abbey Hotel yesterday afternoon?' asked Ravenscroft, deciding to change the direction of his questioning. 'We understand that you had a meeting there with your client.'

'That is indeed so. I had some papers regarding the probate of the estate that I wanted Mr Fincher to sign as soon as possible.'

'According to a witness, the two of you argued, and you left rather suddenly.'

'That is not true. Mr Fincher and I had a most amicable meeting, lasting some ten minutes or so, and then I left the hotel. Your informant is clearly mistaken,' answered Snaith, adopting a more confident air.

'Did you send your client a letter, asking him to meet you that evening?'

'No. Why would I have wanted to send my client a letter when I had only recently spoken to him?'

'So you did not meet with Adam Pendleton yesterday evening?'

'I have just said that I did not write such a letter, nor did I see my client again that day. Where is all this leading, Ravenscroft? You have clearly got things rather confused here.'

'It might interest you to know that Mr Pendleton went out to meet someone last night, and that he has not returned to the Abbey Hotel. His bed has not been slept in.'

'I see,' remarked Snaith, suddenly adopting a more conciliatory manner. 'My client has gone missing, you say?'

'So it would appear.'

'This is most serious.'

'As he left his luggage behind in his room, it seems that he fully intended to return,' said Crabb.

'Can you think of anywhere in the vicinity where Pendleton might have gone?

'No.'

'Did he ever mention to you that he was about to pay a visit to anyone in the area?' persisted Ravenscroft.

'No, he said nothing on that quarter.'

'We have to find Mr Pendleton as soon as possible. We will make urgent enquiries, and once we have found him, you can be assured that we will have words with you again, Mr Snaith. This matter is far from over. In the meantime, if you hear from your client, then you must contact us as soon as possible.'

'Of course. I fully understand.'

'We will resolve this matter Mr Snaith, of that you can be assured.'

* * *

'He knows more than he is letting on,' said Ravenscroft as he and Crabb walked away from the solicitor's offices.

'The man is guilty as anything,' said Crabb.

'I am sure that he knew perfectly well that the real Rupert Fincher was dead. When the old woman died, he saw an opportunity to gain her estate. His accomplice was this Adam Pendleton. Once Pendleton had claimed Maud Fincher's inheritance, pretending to be her long-lost cousin, then I am confident that he and Snaith would have split the money between them. But Snaith is correct when he says that it will be the deuce to prove such allegations.'

'That makes it all the more important to find Pendleton.'

'Indeed,' said Ravenscroft. 'Did you see how Snaith's demeanour changed when we informed him that Pendleton was missing? The colour almost drained from his cheeks and he adopted a far less aggressive tone.'

'Perhaps he has killed Pendleton and he thought we suspected him,' suggested Crabb.

'Why would he have done away with his partner in crime? Without Pendleton, there is no claimant to the estate, and no legacy to inherit. No, I can see no advantage in Snaith deciding to get rid of Pendleton.'

'Unless the two men fell out, and Pendleton was threatening to expose Snaith for his duplicity,' said Crabb.

'No, I am afraid I do not see that either, but all this is idle speculation. Pendleton has gone missing and we need to find him as soon as possible. If we can extract a confession from him that implicates Snaith, then I will be well satisfied. We will make enquiries of the local cabmen. If Pendleton left the Abbey Hotel last night he might have requested a cab to take him to his destination.'

'I think Police Constable Coombs from the Malvern Station is trying to attract our attention, sir,' interrupted Crabb observing that a young uniformed officer was signalling to them from lower down Church Street.

'I wonder what he wants,' said Ravenscroft, quickening his pace.

'What is it, Coombs?' said Crabb, as the constable rushed up the steep road towards the two detectives.

'You best come quickly,' said the out-of-breath officer.

'Take your time, Coombs,' urged Ravenscroft.

'We have found a body at the Swan Pool, sir.'

'Pendleton?' said Crabb, looking at Ravenscroft.

'Doctor Cranbrook is there now with the body,' continued the constable.

'Cranbrook? What the devil is he doing there!'

CHAPTER TEN

'Lead the way, Constable,' said Ravenscroft, as he and Crabb made their way into the Priory Gardens.

'Doctor Cranbrook discovered the body, sir, floating in the Swan Pool,' said Coombs.

As Ravenscroft drew near to the pool, he found Cranbrook, another uniformed officer and two bystanders clustered around the body of a dead man.

'Doctor Cranbrook,' acknowledged Ravenscroft, bending down to examine the body.

Cranbrook looked nervous when he saw Ravenscroft. 'I was walking in the park a few minutes ago,' he explained, 'when I happened to notice him floating in the water. I sent for assistance to the local police station.'

'I have had a look inside his coat pocket, sir, but there is no identification on him,' said the policeman.

'Oh, I know who he is. His name is Adam Pendleton. He has been staying at the Abbey Hotel,' answered Ravenscroft. 'How do you think he died, Doctor?'

'He has taken a nasty blow to the back of his head, just there,' indicated Cranbrook. 'I would guess that after he sustained that blow, someone pushed the body into the pool.'

'It looks quite deliberate. I doubt if it could have been an accident,' said Ravenscroft. 'How long do you think he has been dead?'

'It is difficult to say. It probably happened yesterday evening,' said Cranbrook.

'We know that the man probably left the hotel sometime after eight yesterday evening. He was evidently meeting his attacker here. As it was dark at the time, I doubt that we will find a witness. Crabb, go through his pockets and see if you can find anything.'

'Yes, sir,' said Crabb, kneeling down.

'Was there anyone else in the park when you came here this morning?' enquired Ravenscroft.

'No,' replied Cranbrook.

'May I enquire, Doctor, what you were doing here at this relatively early hour?'

'I was just returning from visiting a patient.'

'Who was that, Doctor?'

'Look, Ravenscroft, surely you don't suspect me of killing this man? It is plain that he was killed last night.'

'Coombs, take a look in those bushes and see if you can find anything that might have been used to inflict the blow,' instructed Ravenscroft, ignoring the last remark.

'Yes, sir,' replied the constable.

'Now, Doctor, you were about to give me the name of your patient,' said Ravenscroft, turning towards Cranbrook.

'If you must know, it was Mrs Moncrief in Malvern Link.'

'I see. Why did you not catch the train back to Colwall after your visit?'

'I had to go to the chemist's in Great Malvern to collect some supplies. As it was such a pleasant morning, I decided to walk through the Priory Gardens.'

'Thank you, Doctor.'

'There is nothing in his pockets, sir,' said Crabb.

'Inspector!' called out Coombs. 'I think you should see this.'

Ravenscroft and Crabb moved across to the nearby undergrowth where the policeman was holding up a large stone in his hand.

'This was lying just by this bush, on the side of the path,' said the constable.

'Do you think this could this have been used to strike the man, Doctor?' asked Ravenscroft.

'It is highly likely,' replied Cranbrook. 'It would appear to be the right size.'

'Thank you, Doctor. Are you alright?' asked Ravenscroft noticing that the man's left hand had begun to shake.

'Yes, yes, it is just a delayed reaction to discovering the body, I suppose. It will pass in a moment. I will be fine. Would you like me to accompany the body to the morgue? I could make a further examination of the body, before I issue a death certificate,' offered Cranbrook.

'Yes, that would be helpful,' answered Ravenscroft. 'Coombs, would you arrange this?'

'Yes, sir.'

'If I find anything of importance I will of course contact you as soon as possible,' said Cranbrook.

'Thank you, Doctor,' said Ravenscroft, before he and Crabb walked away from the scene.

'Terrible business,' muttered Crabb.

'Yes, it was a pity that letter was not on his person. His attacker must have used it to lure him here to the Swan Pool, where he or she killed the poor man, before removing it from his pocket. This is a strange business, Tom. Why would anyone want to kill Pendleton?'

'Perhaps there is another claimant to the estate?' suggested Crabb.

'You mean the next in line inherits? But you are forgetting one thing: there is no heir. Rupert Fincher was the last of his family, as far as we know.'

'What will happen to Maud Fincher's estate now?'

'I would think any money would be put into the jurisdiction of the Crown, where I presume it would remain until some other person lays claim to it in the future.'

'It was rather strange that it was Cranbrook who discovered the body,' said Crabb.

'Yes, but it might be just a coincidence that he was here this morning. We can certainly confirm or disprove his account by talking with Janet Moncrief. He may be telling us the truth when he said he came this way because he wanted a pleasant walk. Almost certainly Pendleton was killed yesterday evening. If Cranbrook was the killer it does not make sense that he would then return to the scene of the crime the following morning. A killer would usually want to be as far away as possible from where the crime was committed. No, it does not make sense at all for Cranbrook to have killed Pendleton. Anyway, what reason would he have for doing so?

'Did you see how his hand was shaking?'

'Yes. Was he overcome by his sudden discovery of the body, as he claimed, or does he have some medical condition? He certainly seemed very nervous and unsettled.'

'Surely a medical man is used to dead bodies? I thought they had to do anatomy and all that at medical school.'

'You would have thought so. He could be taking some kind of medication, which is not suiting him.'

'So what do we do now, sir?'

'If we want to know who killed Adam Pendleton then we must try and find out more about the fellow. Where did he originate from? At the moment, Marcus Snaith remains our chief suspect. I am sure that it was Snaith who put Pendleton forward to impersonate Rupert Fincher. We know that the two men had an argument yesterday afternoon. Could Snaith have then decided to get rid of Pendleton before the young man confessed to the deception? I think we should go back to the Abbey Hotel and inform Mr Collins that his guest will not be returning, and while we are there I want to take a closer look at the young man's personal effects.'

* * *

'Nothing but collection of clothes,' remarked Ravenscroft staring down at the bundle of garments on the bed. 'And not of the best; like his rather worn case, they have all seen much better days. This would suggest that our Mr Pendleton was a man of fairly limited means.'

'There is his brush and comb set, but there is no lettering on that,' said Crabb.

'Damn it! Try the lining of his case; something may have slipped down there.'

'Nothing,' replied Crabb, after a few moments had elapsed.

'This is all very frustrating. You would have thought that the man would have carried some papers with him that would have enabled us to have identified him. Wait a moment. There is the spirit flask. That was how we discovered his identity,' said Ravenscroft, picking up and examining the silver container. 'No, there is just the name, although there is some small lettering on the base, next to a picture of an anchor.'

'That's Birmingham,' remarked Crabb. 'That's the Birmingham hallmark.'

'How do you know that, Tom?' asked Ravenscroft, surprised.

'A great uncle of mine had a silver trophy, given to him for some achievement at an agricultural show I believe. I remember him showing it to us and saying that it had been made in Birmingham.'

'There is another name here, if I can just make it out — Withering and Co.'

'That must be the maker.'

'So this flask was made in Birmingham by Withering and Co?'

'It would appear so.'

'Then we need to make our way to Great Malvern Railway Station as soon as possible and take the next train to Birmingham. If we can track down the maker there, he might be able to tell us more about its owner, and more importantly provide us with an address. Perhaps the answer to this crime lies in finding out more about this Adam Pendleton.'

* * *

Two hours later, after travelling to Birmingham on the main Hereford to Birmingham line, and after visiting Birmingham Central Library to consult the local Directory, Ravenscroft and Crabb made their way along the bustling main street of the great metropolis.

'It is a lot busier than Ledbury or Malvern,' remarked Crabb.

'More like London, with all its noise and people. Have you ever been here before?' asked Ravenscroft.

'No, sir, and I can't say that I am particularly anxious to remain here longer than we have to.'

'Ah, here we are. If we turn off now, we should find Withering and Co somewhere on the left, according to the map.'

'That must be it.' Crabb indicated a large glass-fronted shop.

'There are plenty of trophies and silverware in the window. We must have the right place. Let's see if they can tell us anything relating to the owner of this flask,' said Ravenscroft. He reached out for the door handle, only to find it opened instead by a tall gentleman wearing a frock coat and top hat.

'Good day to you, gentlemen,' said the doorman.

'Good day,' replied Ravenscroft as he and Crabb entered the shop.

'I will see if Mr Withering is free to see you,' said the doorman, indicating with a flourish that Crabb and Ravenscroft were to follow him into the interior of the premises.

'Thank you,' said Ravenscroft.

'Two gentlemen to see you, Mr Withering,' said the doorman, speaking to a tall bald-headed man, sporting a large drooping moustache and long side whiskers, who was busily inspecting the inside of a pocket watch, on the other side of a large oak counter.

'Good day to you, gentlemen. Joseph Withering at your service. I do not believe that I have had the pleasure of seeing you in our emporium before today. How can I be of assistance to you? We have plenty of fine pocket watches to adorn the most colourful of waistcoats, elegant time pieces that would not look out of place in any room in the house, silver and plated items of the utmost quality, and all reasonably priced for the discerning pocket.'

'None of those, thank you, Mr Withering,' said Ravenscroft, thinking that if he did not interrupt the shopkeeper's flow of words he and Crabb would be there for the remainder of the day. 'I wonder what you can tell me about this flask. I believe it is one of yours.'

'It may well be,' said Withering, taking the item from Ravenscroft, and fixing a magnifying glass to his eye so that he could examine the piece.

'Well?' said Ravenscroft after a few seconds had elapsed.

'I am happy to confirm your assumption. The said item was indeed made by our company. Perhaps you are looking to have a similar flask made?'

'No, Mr Withering. We require some information regarding its owner.'

'Oh, I am afraid I cannot do that,' said Withering displaying an air of disdain as he placed the flask firmly down on the counter. 'That is a confidential matter between its owner and our company. Discretion is our watchword here at Withering and Co.'

'I appreciate your position Mr Withering, but we are police officers. The owner of this flask was brutally murdered last night in Great Malvern, and we would like you to tell us all you know about this man.'

'Oh, dear me, dear me, that is most sad,' said Withering. 'Malvern you say? Such a delightful town. I have an old aunt of mine who took the waters there quite recently, and she speaks quite highly of it.

'I remember this flask. It was ordered by a number of Mr Pendleton's cricketing friends — at the Bournville Cricket Club — to be presented to him on the occasion of his twenty-first birthday, if I recall correctly.'

'Excellent. Do you have an address for Mr Pendleton?' asked Ravenscroft.

'Ah well, that would depend on whether the flask was sent directly to Mr Pendleton, or whether the order was placed by another gentleman. If the latter is the case, then I do not think we can be of assistance to you.'

'Either would be useful.'

'Let me go and consult my records. You are?'

'Detective Inspector Ravenscroft.'

'If you would kindly wait here a moment, Inspector, I should not keep you waiting for long.'

Ravenscroft smiled as the man disappeared from view into an inner office.

'Nice place,' whispered Crabb, looking at the numerous clocks on the walls.

'Perhaps you would feel inclined to purchase a gift for Mrs Crabb,' suggested Ravenscroft light-heartedly.

'Not at these prices,' replied Crabb, studying one of the price labels. 'What about Mrs Ravenscroft?'

'I think she would have to choose it herself. I am hopeless at these things.'

'Ah, here we are,' said Withering after some minutes had elapsed, emerging from the inner office and carrying a large open ledger in his hands. 'Fortune is shining on you. It seems that we did indeed send the flask to Mr Pendleton.'

'That is good news.'

'I will write the address out for you,' offered Withering.

'I would be obliged. You sell many of these items?'

'The flask is one of our most popular lines. There we are.' Withering laid down his pen.

'Smethwick. Where is Smethwick?' enquired Ravenscroft.

'It is a small town to the west of Birmingham, some three or four miles. I am sure that the people at the railway station will be able tell you when the next train leaves.'

'Thank you, Mr Withering, you have been of great value to us in our investigations,' said Ravenscroft about to take his leave.

'Do not forget the flask, sir.'

'Thank you,' said Ravenscroft, picking up the item and placing it is his pocket. 'We will see that his next of kin takes rightful possession of it.'

* * *

'Thirty-eight Grange Road,' repeated Ravenscroft, as he and Crabb walked down the street of uniformed terraced houses later that afternoon.

'Over there, sir.'

Ravenscroft tapped on the door. 'I fear we will be the bringers of bad news. We need to tread carefully.'

'I can hear a child crying,' said Crabb after a few moments had passed.

Ravenscroft tapped again, and presently the door was opened by a young woman, who was holding a young infant in her arms.

'Good afternoon, madam,' said Ravenscroft removing his hat. 'I believe that this might be the residence of Mr Adam Pendleton?'

'Yes,' replied the woman. 'But I am afraid that my husband is not here at the present time. He is away on business. I am Alice Pendleton. Can I help you gentlemen?'

Ravenscroft noticed that the woman's face was worn and drawn, as if the circumstances of her situation had not been kind to her, and he knew that the next few minutes would be difficult. 'It is you we have come to see, Mrs Pendleton. We have some rather bad news concerning your husband.'

'Oh no!' cried out the woman, with a sudden look of pain in her eyes.

'My name is Detective Inspector Ravenscroft and this is Detective Sergeant Crabb. May we please enter? We will not detain you long,' said Ravenscroft, choosing his words carefully, and yet hating his own inadequacy.

'No, no!' repeated the woman clutching her child closer to her body, as she stepped away from the entrance.

Ravenscroft and Crabb entered and cautiously followed the woman into a small drawing room.

'Hello, mister,' said a young boy of not more than six years of age, who stared up at the detective.

'Hello, young man — and what is your name?'

'John. John Pendleton,' replied the boy proudly.

'That is a fine name indeed,' smiled Ravenscroft.

'Do you play cricket, mister?'

'Unfortunately not.'

'My father plays cricket for the Bournville Cricket Club,' said the boy proudly.

'And do you want to be a cricketer when you grow up?'

'I hope so.'

'John, go to your room, please,' said the woman in a voice that seemed close to breaking.

'Oh, Mummy,' protested the boy with a look of disappointment.

'John, do as I tell you,' retorted Alice Pendleton.

The boy looked at his mother and began to cry, before hastily leaving the room.

'I am very sorry to be the bringer of such bad news,' mumbled Ravenscroft before coughing and clearing his voice. 'I wonder do you have a photograph of your husband?'

The woman seized a silver frame on the mantelpiece and thrust it into the detective's hands, with a look of desperation on her face.

'Yes, it is the same man,' confirmed Ravenscroft. 'I am sorry to tell you that your husband is dead, Mrs—'

'No, no!'

Ravenscroft and Crabb stood in silence, looking down at the threadbare carpet, not wanting to speak as they listened to the woman's sobs.

After some moments had elapsed, Alice Pendleton drew her sleeve across her eyes. 'I apologise, I am neglecting my manners,' she said in a quiet voice.

'No, I can assure you that it is alright,' said Ravenscroft, forcing a strained smile.

'Please, sit down.'

'Thank you.'

'You say Adam is dead? How, how did it happen?' said the mother trying to hold back more tears, as she looked down at the small baby in her arms.

'Your husband was found this morning in Great Malvern. It appears that he had sustained a blow to the back of his head late yesterday evening,' said Ravenscroft, finding it difficult to use the right words. 'Apparently he had been staying at the Abbey Hotel at the time.'

'I don't understand,' replied Alice Pendleton, giving the detective a look of incomprehension. 'Great Malvern, you say?'

'That is correct, Mrs Pendleton.'

'But my husband is in Manchester. How can he have died in Malvern?'

'Can I ask what your husband's employment is?' asked Ravenscroft, perplexed.

'He is a commercial salesman for a chocolate company.'

'When did you last see your husband?'

'On Monday afternoon. He said he was going to Manchester to visit a number of clients there,' said Alice, a pained expression on her face.

'When did your husband say he would return?'

'Today. I was expecting him later this afternoon. There must be some mistake in all this. You are obviously confusing this dead man with my husband. I am expecting him any moment now. You will see for yourself.'

'I have seen the dead man with my own eyes — he is the same man in that photograph you showed me. We were able to identify him because this flask was in his luggage,' said Ravenscroft, producing the item from his coat pocket and passing it over to the distressed woman. 'Perhaps you would be kind enough to identify this as your husband's property.'

Alice Pendleton stared down at the flask before dropping it on to the floor and sobbing loudly.

Ravenscroft looked at Crabb, removed his spectacles and cleaned them on his handkerchief, feeling that he had no desire to continue with the questioning, but knowing that he would have to proceed further if he was to arrive at the truth.

The baby began to cry, as the mantle clock struck the hour of four.

'Before your husband left on Monday, did he receive any letter or telegram?' asked Ravenscroft.

'Yes, a letter did arrive.'

'Did your husband say who it was from, this letter?'

'No, he just read it, and then he said he would have to travel to Manchester and that he would probably return today,' sobbed Alice Pendleton as she looked down at her baby and rocked it gently in her arms.

'Do you have this letter now?'

'No, my husband put it in his coat pocket.'

'That is a pity. So did your husband not say anything at all about going to Great Malvern?'

'I've told you, he said he was going to Manchester,' retorted Alice. 'Why are you asking me all these questions?'

'I am sorry, Mrs Pendleton, but if we are to catch your husband's killer, I need to know as much as I can about his movements,' said Ravenscroft in a quiet voice, hating himself for his persistence. 'Does the name Rupert Fincher mean anything to you? Perhaps your husband mentioned the name Fincher?'

'No, it means nothing to me.'

'Do you know if your husband ever visited the town of Cirencester?'

'No. Hush, my baby, hush.'

'Did he ever mention Colwall?'

'No. I don't understand all these questions. I think I would like you to go now. My children have need of me,' said Alice Pendleton, the tears still wet on her cheeks.

'Yes, of course,' said Ravenscroft standing up. 'I am very sorry for the death of your husband. Please accept my deepest condolences. Rest assured, Mrs Pendleton, that we will find your husband's killer and bring him to justice.'

'That is no comfort to me,' replied the mother, looking down at her child once more. 'Who will provide for us now that Adam is no longer with us?'

Ravenscroft said nothing as he twisted his hat round in his hands.

The door opened and the boy entered. 'Please, Mummy, where is Daddy?'

'John, I told you to stay in your room,' cried Alice Pendleton.

'Daddy said he would be home today.'

'Daddy will not be coming home to us.'

'Mummy, why are you crying?'

'I cannot help it my son. Come here.'

The boy ran up to his mother and buried his sobbing face in the folds of her dress.

'We will see ourselves out. I will see to it that the undertakers make contact with you,' said Ravenscroft uneasily, as he and Crabb began to take their leave.

'I suppose I will have to inform his uncle,' mumbled Alice.

'His uncle?' asked Ravenscroft.

'Yes, Adam's uncle, Mr Snaith.'

'Mr Snaith?' said a startled Ravenscroft.

'Yes, Mr Marcus Snaith. He is a solicitor in Malvern. He is Adam's uncle . . .'

CHAPTER ELEVEN

FRIDAY

'So, Marcus Snaith and Adam Pendleton are related,' said Ravenscroft, as he and Crabb made their way along Belle Vue Terrace on the following morning.

'It is clear that the solicitor took advantage of the situation once he learned that Miss Fincher's real heir was dead, by getting his nephew to impersonate Rupert Fincher,' suggested Crabb.

'Yes it was a very clever plan, and it will be interesting to see what Mr Snaith has to say for himself,' said Ravenscroft, pushing open the door that he knew would eventually bring them to the offices of Maltravers, Wells and Snaith. 'But first we have to negotiate these wretched stairs. Give me the path up to St Ann's Well any day.'

'Good morning, gentlemen,' said the clerk looking up from his ledger as the two detectives entered the attic rooms.

'We wish to see Mr Snaith on urgent business,' said Ravenscroft.

'I am afraid Mr Snaith is presently engaged with a client. If you would care to take a seat, I am sure he will not be long. In fact I think I can hear them now.'

‘Well Snaith you know where I am,’ said a familiar voice from down the corridor.

‘I can assure you, Mr Fanshawe, that I will give the matter my most urgent attention,’ replied Snaith.

‘Be sure you do, Snaith. Time is of the essence. I am anxious to proceed with this matter as soon as possible,’ said Fanshawe, entering the outer room. He did not seem alarmed when he saw the detectives. ‘Inspector Ravenscroft. Sergeant Crabb.’

‘Good morning to you, Mr Fanshawe.’

‘I trust you have recovered from the follies of Wednesday evening, Inspector?’

‘Indeed,’ smiled Ravenscroft.

‘Well, Snaith, there is work to be done. I wish you all good day,’ said Fanshawe as he left.

‘Ravenscroft,’ sighed Snaith, ‘there is nothing I can add further to our previous conversation.’

‘Oh, but I think there is a great deal we need to talk about Mr Snaith, in particular, your nephew, Adam Pendleton.’

Snaith gave a look of startled surprise. ‘You had best come into my office.’

‘We now know that Adam Pendleton was your nephew, and that you put him up to impersonating Rupert Fincher,’ said Ravenscroft, as he and Crabb sat down in the chairs placed before the solicitor’s desk.

‘I am sure I don’t know what you are talking about.’

‘When you learned of the death of your client, Maud Fincher, I have no doubt that you made enquiries in Cirencester regarding her cousin, Rupert Fincher.’ Ravenscroft spoke with confidence. ‘Once you discovered that this gentleman had died some eight years ago, you saw an opportunity to obtain the estate by getting your nephew, Adam Pendleton, to claim that he was the rightful heir.’

‘This is all fanciful,’ replied Snaith, still shaken.

‘Mr Snaith, Adam Pendleton was found dead yesterday morning. Do you still deny that he was your nephew?’

Snaith’s face grew ashen, but he did not speak.

'Yesterday,' went on Ravenscroft, 'my sergeant and I visited the poor widow's house in Smethwick. She was able to confirm that the dead man was indeed her husband. Furthermore she told us that you were Adam Pendleton's uncle. There is no use denying it, Snaith.

'We know that Adam Pendleton received a letter from you last Monday afternoon, informing him of the situation, and giving him instructions to come to Malvern as soon as possible,' pronounced Ravenscroft. 'Do I have to bring his poor widow to Malvern to identify you as Pendleton's uncle?'

Snaith said nothing as he stared down at the papers on his desk.

'What I really want to know is, did you and your nephew plan all this weeks ago?'

'No,' said Snaith adamantly.

'Did you cause Maud Fincher's death, before bringing your plan to fruition?' said Ravenscroft, raising his voice.

'No, this is absurd. I learned about Maud Fincher's death when I read about it in the local newspaper. Neither I nor my nephew had anything to do with her death. The suggestion is quite ridiculous.'

'So you now admit that Adam Pendleton was your nephew?'

'Yes,' sighed Snaith, glaring at Ravenscroft.

'And do you now admit that it was you who asked him to impersonate Rupert Fincher?'

The solicitor said nothing.

'When did you last see your nephew?' asked Ravenscroft.

'It was on Wednesday afternoon, at the Abbey Hotel.'

'When the argument took place between you.'

'There was no argument, as I told you before.'

'I think your nephew was telling you that he wanted nothing more to do with this matter, and that you tried to persuade him to continue. That was what the argument was about, was it not?'

'No. You don't know what you are talking about, Inspector.'

'Then perhaps you could enlighten us as to what your disagreement was really about?' persisted Ravenscroft.

'Adam was anxious to get back to his family in Smethwick. I urged him to remain for a day or two longer, until things settled down, and we could then proceed.'

'Proceed with what?' demanded Ravenscroft.

'With lodging the claim on the estate,' replied Snaith reluctantly.

'I think you then sent your nephew a letter, that afternoon, telling him to meet you by the Swan Pool later that evening after it was dark.'

'This is complete nonsense.'

'I think you then had a further argument at the pool, things became heated between you, and that you hit your nephew on the back of his head.'

'This is all wrong, Inspector,' protested Snaith. 'Why would I want to kill my own nephew?'

'Why indeed? Because he said he wanted nothing more to do with your crooked deception, and because he threatened that he would expose you to the authorities,' said Ravenscroft. 'If your scheme were made public, you would be totally discredited.'

'No, no, this is not true. I never met my nephew by the pool. I never wrote him a letter. Don't you think I regret bringing him here? I would never have involved him in all of this had I known he would be killed,' replied Snaith with a cry of anguish. 'I had nothing to do with this, God help me.'

'I doubt that the good Lord will be in a forgiving mood as far as you are concerned,' retorted Ravenscroft. 'If you had told us the truth before our last visit, your nephew might have been saved.'

'I know, you don't have to tell me that now,' said the solicitor, bringing his hand before his eyes.

'So if you did not kill your nephew, then who did?'

'I don't know.'

'Was there anyone else involved in your scheme?'

'No, of course not.'

'Then who do you think killed him, Mr Snaith?'

'I don't know. The will names Rupert Fincher as the sole beneficiary. There is no one else.'

'And now both Rupert Fincher and your nephew are dead.'

'Look, Inspector, what benefit would I have gained if the only claimant was dead? The money will now go to the Crown, where it will rot away with no one left to claim it.'

'That all seems very logical, Mr Snaith, but I still maintain that it was you who killed your nephew when he threatened to expose your deception,' Ravenscroft persisted.

'Think what you like, Inspector. I did not kill my nephew. It is up to you to prove otherwise. If on the other hand you accept that I am innocent of this crime, then get out there and find out who really killed my nephew. I want to see this killer bought to justice as much as you do,' pleaded Snaith.

Ravenscroft looked at the solicitor without replying.

'For goodness' sake, man, say something,' said an anguished Snaith.

'That will be all for now, Mr Snaith,' said Ravenscroft quickly rising from his chair. 'I advise you not to leave Malvern while we are proceeding with our investigation.'

'I have no intention of leaving the town. I want this killer caught, Inspector. My nephew did not deserve to die so brutally.'

'Before we take our leave, may I ask what Mr Fanshawe was doing here this morning?' asked Ravenscroft.

'That is entirely between Mr Fanshawe and me. It is none of your business,' replied Snaith, recovering some of his former assertive manner.

'May I remind you, Mr Snaith, that we are conducting an enquiry into what look like two murders, those of Adam Pendleton and Maud Fincher. If we find the killer of Miss Fincher, we find the killer of your nephew. I will ask you once again — what was the purpose of Mr Fanshawe's visit?'

'Mr Fanshawe has expressed an interest in purchasing Miss Fincher's former property, Claremont. That is all.'

‘He seems quite anxious about the matter,’ remarked Crabb.

‘Do you know why Mr Fanshawe wishes to undertake such a purchase?’ asked Ravenscroft.

‘He did not say. Of course, I will have to tell him that I am not able to help him, now that there is no legal heir to the estate.’

‘Although such a property might be sold and the funds sent to the Exchequer?’

‘That might be possible.’

‘Well Mr Snaith, we will bid you good day for now, but be assured that I will probably have need to talk with you again,’ said Ravenscroft.

‘Just catch the man who committed this terrible crime,’ pleaded Snaith.

‘We will do our best. In the meantime, there is a destitute widow and two small children in Smethwick who are in need of your financial and moral assistance.’

Snaith said nothing as the two detectives left the room.

* * *

‘If you ask me, that man is as guilty as anything,’ remarked Crabb, as he and Ravenscroft climbed into the trap. ‘He and his nephew brought about the death of Maud Fincher so that Adam Pendleton could pretend to be Rupert Fincher and they could then lay claim to the poor woman’s estate. Then Pendleton got cold feet and wanted to pull out of the enterprise, the two men quarrelled, and Snaith killed him to keep him quiet.’

‘You could well be correct, Tom. It certainly points that way. However I have my doubts. We certainly know that the two men were trying to obtain the inheritance, but what advantage would Snaith have in killing his own nephew? That would have put paid to any hope of his gaining the money.’

‘I still think he killed him to stop Pendleton from talking.’

'If you are correct, we will have the devil to prove it,' sighed Ravenscroft.

'What was Mr Fanshawe doing there? Do you believe all that about him wanting to buy Maud Fincher's property?'

'Yes, that was certainly most interesting. What would Fanshawe want with Claremont?'

'He is a builder, sir.'

'You mean he may have wanted to buy the property and improve it, possibly for himself?' replied Ravenscroft, thinking out loud. 'I cannot see that it is in an enviable or valuable position. There is no gold in the Malvern Hills, at least none that I know about.'

'So what do we do now?'

'Well, I would certainly like to speak with Mr Fanshawe and see why he wants to buy Claremont. He might have brought undue pressure to bear on Maud Fincher to sell the property to him, in which case we cannot rule out the possibility that he may have caused her death, or that he is involved with Marcus Snaith in some way. But that can wait until later in the morning. I want to visit the Moncriefs again. I am curious to know if their real name is Williamson and discover the reason why they left Shipston-on-Stour. Furthermore, Doctor Cranbrook said he had just visited Janet Moncrief when he discovered the body of Adam Pendleton, so we also need to confirm his alibi.'

'You think it is more than just a coincidence that Cranbrook was both treating Maud Fincher and that it was him that found Pendleton's body?'

'I don't know, Tom, but I would like to find out if the good doctor was telling us the truth.'

* * *

'Inspector Ravenscroft, how nice it is to see you again,' said Janet Moncrief, opening the front door of her house.

'Good morning to you Mrs Moncrief. My sergeant and I would be grateful for a few minutes of your time,' said Ravenscroft.

'Yes, of course. Do please come in,' said Janet Moncrief opening the door wider, and indicating that the two policemen were to enter. 'I am afraid my husband is not here at the present time, although I am expecting him in another hour or so.'

'Actually, it is you we have come to see.'

'Oh, that sounds very serious,' laughed Janet Moncrief. 'Do please take a seat, gentlemen. Can I offer you some refreshment? Some tea or cordial perhaps?'

'That will not be necessary, thank you,' replied Ravenscroft, easing himself into the end seat of the sofa, as Crabb took out his pocketbook. 'You may have heard of the unfortunate death of a young man yesterday morning in Great Malvern.'

'Yes, I was just reading about it in the newspaper. What a terrible business.'

'It was Doctor Cranbrook who discovered the body at the Swan Pool. He informed us that he had been visiting you earlier that morning. Can you confirm that fact for us, Mrs Moncrief?' asked Crabb.

'Well, yes, I am happy to say that is correct. He is such a nice young man, Doctor Cranbrook. I do not know what I would do without him. Surely you don't suspect him of killing this young man? The idea is quite ridiculous.'

'We have to confirm his whereabouts before his discovery of the body. It is just police routine, I can assure you. May I be so bold as to ask the reason for his visit yesterday morning?'

'Really, Inspector, that is a matter of confidence between the doctor and his patient,' laughed Janet Moncrief.

'Of course, please forgive me,' apologised Ravenscroft, fearing that he had been indiscreet.

'I find the strain caused by my mission in life to be very debilitating at times. After each séance I feel physically quite drained. Doctor Cranbrook prescribed a tonic as a restorative.'

'Yes, your work must be quite arduous.'

'Silas Crabbit and his companions are inclined to impose themselves on one. There is little I can do to resist them. Why, it was only yesterday that I spoke once again with your sister, Anne. She says that she knows that you are shortly to be faced with an important decision, a decision that will change your life quite dramatically, Inspector , but she informs me that you will overcome these difficulties in time, and that all will be well with you,' said Janet Moncrief, talking in a soothing voice as she sat down on the sofa next to Ravenscroft. 'Nevertheless, she also said that you will face great danger and that you would need to be careful.'

'I have to tell you, Mrs Moncrief, that my sergeant has made enquiries in Shipston-on-Stour,' replied an uneasy Ravenscroft, clearing his throat.

'And what enquiries might they be?' asked Janet Moncrief, looking quite untroubled.

'We believe that you and your husband went by the name of Williamson during the few months that you lived in Shipston,' said Crabb, looking up from his notebook.

'I am sure I do not know what you are talking about, Constable.'

'Sergeant, Mrs Moncrief,' corrected Crabb.

'Please forgive me, Sergeant. As I said, I have never heard of anyone called Williamson living in Shipston.'

'You would not deny that you and your husband lived in Shipston? You admitted as such when I first visited you.'

'Felix and I certainly did live in Shipston for a few months, but I can assure you that we did not call ourselves Williamson. May I ask what it is that these people are said to have done?'

'They tried to establish a church of spiritualism,' continued Crabb.

'I do not think that can be so. You must be mistaken, Sergeant. Had that been the case I am sure that Felix and I would have known these people.'

'I have spoken to several of the residents there,' said Crabb, 'and they all say that the Williamsons match your appearance. The local vicar was particularly helpful to our enquiries. We believe you were forced to leave the town because of several improprieties.'

'Oh dear me, what tittle-tattle people indulge in.'

'So you deny that your name was Williamson and you were forced to leave Shipston because many of the people there objected to your activities?' asked Ravenscroft.

'Sometimes it is difficult for people to accept that we only want to help them, by bringing new hope and relief into their lives,' replied Janet Moncrief, ignoring the detective's last question. 'But not everyone wishes to be helped in this way. There are many that would speak out against us.'

'Oh? Why is that?'

'People often fear the unknown. They seek safety in what they know. In order to become a believer one needs to open one's heart and mind. That is the only way to salvation. I believe, Inspector, that you have already opened your heart. Your sister has spoken to you. For years you have denied the inevitable, and it is only now that you can accept the truth.'

'Mrs Moncrief, I fear we are moving away from the reason for our visit today,' said Ravenscroft, feeling distinctly unsettled by the spiritualist's words. 'This is a very pleasant house in which you reside. May I be so bold as to enquire how you manage to live here, when it appears that neither of you is engaged in any gainful employment?'

'I can assure you that our mission on this earth is our full-time occupation. We rent the house. My husband has a small annuity, and occasionally one or two of our followers have supported us with financial gifts.'

'People like Colonel Mortimer and Mrs Tinniswood?' suggested Ravenscroft.

'Oh dear me, Inspector, you would not expect me to betray such confidences.'

'No, but you are endeavouring to build a church here in Malvern Link? I understand that you hope that Mr Fanshawe will become your benefactor.'

'Mr Fanshawe has kindly mentioned that he may be able to help us in that endeavour. If we were able to build such a church here amongst the good people of Malvern and the surrounding areas, then it would certainly be the pinnacle of all we have been trying to achieve.'

'I do not believe that there are many such churches in the country.'

'We are pioneers. Where we lead, others with follow,' said Janet Moncrief, speaking with enthusiasm.

'I do not think Mr Fanshawe is all that prepared to carry out such an undertaking,' said Crabb.

'Mr Fanshawe is not yet a true believer. He remains a sceptic at present, but we believe that once he has experienced more of our work, he will be become a convert and be only too anxious to assist us in reaching out to the unbelievers.'

'And Maud Fincher? Was she one of your true believers?' asked Ravenscroft.

'Of course. We were able to help her a great deal.'

'So much so that she was afraid Crabbit was about to kill her?'

'We cannot help it if sometimes our spirit friends are a little forthcoming in their demands. As I said earlier, we have little control over the feelings of those in the spirit world. Like the people they have left behind, they can be subject to all kinds of extraneous feelings and thoughts.'

'How long has Silas Crabbit been your spirit guide?'

'Silas first made his presence felt about two years ago.'

'When I asked you and your husband if you could tell us more about Crabbit, you stated that you were unaware from where he had originated,' said Ravenscroft.

'That is so.'

'He never told you where he lived, or how he died?'

'No, I am afraid I cannot help you there.'

'That I find difficult to believe. You say that all the spirits that you have contact with in the other world are related in some way to the people who attend your séances?'

'That is indeed so.'

'All, except Silas Crabbit?'

'I know you may find this difficult to believe, Inspector, but Silas is my spirit guide. It is through him that we are able to understand what our departed loved ones are saying and feeling.'

'You say that Silas first appeared to you two years ago. In all this time he must have mentioned something that would assist us in finding out more about him.'

'No, I am afraid not, although he has mentioned once or twice something about a cave.'

'A cave? Did he say where this cave was, or what happened to him there?' asked Ravenscroft.

'No, but I know that he was very frightened when he mentioned it, as though something unpleasant had happened to him in this cave.'

'That is interesting. Do you think he had died in the cave?'

'I don't know. I cannot help you anymore. I am very tired. You must excuse me.'

'One final question, Mrs Moncrief, if I may: where were you living at the time when Silas Crabbit first spoke to you?'

'I am not sure.'

'Please, try and remember.'

Janet Moncrief stared hard at Ravenscroft before speaking. 'I think it might have been when we were living in Ombersley.'

'Thank you, Mrs Moncrief.' Ravenscroft rose to his feet. 'I appreciate your time and patience. We will take our leave.'

'Please feel free to call any time that you wish, Inspector. We are all in need of assistance. Anne is there for you. All you need to do is to have the desire to speak with her.'

* * *

'Well, Tom, I don't think we got very far there,' said Ravenscroft, as he and Crabb walked away from the Moncriefs' residence.

'At least she was able to confirm Doctor Cranbrook's story.'

'Yes, it appears that the good doctor was telling us the truth after all. What do you make of Janet Moncrief?'

'She was telling us a lot of nonsense. I don't believe any of that about communicating with the dead.'

'I am inclined to agree with you. The Moncriefs play on people's vulnerability, but the question remains: do they sincerely believe in what they are doing, or are they fabricating the whole thing about these spirits so that they can extract money from their clients?'

'I think they are complete charlatans.'

'I cannot be so sure. We have found no evidence that people have been compelled to give them money against their will.'

'They may just be very clever, and very fortunate that no one has ever bought charges against them.'

'You could be right, Tom. I wanted to know more about this Silas Crabbit. Maud Fincher clearly thought that Crabbit was trying to kill her. Were the Moncriefs trying to extract money from Maud Fincher? If so, and they were unsuccessful, did they then use Crabbit as a means of furthering their aims?'

'This Crabbit spirit is all nonsense. I don't think he ever existed, and then there was this fanciful story about a cave,' said Crabb dismissively.

'Crabbit could well be a work of fiction. Although she seemed quite definite about him dying in a cave. You could almost believe there was some truth in all this spiritualism if you were gullible. Anyway, that is enough of that for the time being. I want to know why Fanshawe is anxious to buy Claremont.'

'Shall we visit him next, sir?' asked Crabb, climbing into the trap.

'No, I think we should go to Claremont first and have a word with the maid, Gladys Brotherton. She may be able to provide us with some information regarding Mr Fanshawe and her late mistress. I just hope that she has not already packed her bags and left.'

* * *

'Good morning to you,' said Ravenscroft, removing his hat, as he and Crabb stood on the doorstep of Claremont.

'Good morning, Inspector,' replied Gladys Brotherton.

'I wonder if we might enter and have a few words with you?' asked Ravenscroft, observing that the maid was dressed in formal black mourning attire.

The maid opened the door wider and the two detectives entered the hallway.

'We will not take up too much of your time, Gladys.' Ravenscroft came straight to the point. 'Did Mr Fanshawe ever call upon Miss Fincher?'

'He came to the séances when they were held here.'

'Did he ever come alone?'

'Yes, two or three times.'

'I wonder if you can recall what the conversation was about between your mistress and Mr Fanshawe?'

'Yes, I remember quite clearly. Mr Fanshawe wanted Miss Fincher to sell him Claremont.' Her tone was matter-of-fact.

'And I gather that Miss Fincher was unwilling to comply with his request?'

'That is indeed so.'

'Do you know why Mr Fanshawe wanted to buy the house?'

'No. He never said, but I know he was quite persistent. I believe that he even increased his offer for the property, but the mistress was adamant that she would not sell. Where else could she go?'

'Quite. And you supported her in this?'

'It was not my place to offer my mistress advice.'

'Did Miss Fincher ever mention to you that there was anything valuable about the property?'

'I don't quite understand your question.'

'That there might be something of extra value that would increase the property's value,' continued Ravenscroft.

'No, the mistress did not speak about these matters, and it was not my place to ask.'

'No doubt you have heard the news concerning Mr Rupert Fincher?'

'Yes, Mr Snaith has written me a letter. It is a terrible business. He seemed quite a nice young man, although of course I only saw him at the funeral. Mr Snaith has asked me to remain here and look after the house until everything is resolved.'

'Are you happy to do that?'

'I would rather seek fresh employment elsewhere, but Mr Snaith was quite insistent that I must remain, so I feel I must comply with his wishes. It is what my late mistress would have wanted. I do not know where all this will end. Perhaps someone will eventually purchase the property,' replied Gladys Brotherton wearily.

'Thank you, Gladys. We will leave you to your duties.'

Ravenscroft and Crabb walked down the path.

'I wonder why Fanshawe wanted to buy this property,' said Ravenscroft turning round and looking up at the building.

'It stands on quite a large piece of land,' remarked Crabb.

'Whatever it was, he seems to have been quite persistent.'

'Indeed. I wonder if he was using the Moncriefs to make the old lady fearful of her life and drive her away.'

'By using Crabbit you mean?'

'Exactly. But I fear we may be clutching at straws here. What was that?'

'What?'

'I thought I heard a sound from behind us, as though someone was there.'

'I did not hear anything, sir.'

'All this spiritualism is making me uneasy. I am beginning to imagine things,' said Ravenscroft. 'Now, Tom, I want you to do something for me. I want to get to the bottom of this Crabbit business. Janet Moncrief claims Silas Crabbit first spoke to her in Ombersley. I want to know if this Crabbit was ever a real person, and if so, whether he lived in Ombersley and what happened to him. If he met an untimely death, it must have been reported in the main Worcester newspaper. I want you to get the next train to Worcester, visit the newspaper office and go through their back copies, starting two years ago and working back. See if you can find anything. Come to the house tomorrow morning.'

'Yes, sir.'

'In the meantime I will go and have a word with Fanshawe. I want to know why he was so insistent in his demands to buy Claremont.'

* * *

'Good morning,' said Ravenscroft addressing the maid who opened the door of Mr Fanshawe's house in Abbey Road. 'Is your master at home?'

'No, sir. He is busy working on one of his properties at present.'

'Oh and where might that be?'

'Further along the road, on the left-hand side. You will see a new house being built,' said the maid pointing.

'Thank you, then I must trust I will find him there.'

After patting his horse, Ravenscroft made his way back along Abbey Road.

'Good morning, my man, I am looking for Mr Fanshawe,' called out Ravenscroft to a workman who was busy laying bricks in the front garden of a half-built house.

'Master be at the back,' replied the man with a brief nod of his head.

Ravenscroft made his way down the side of the house, until he noticed Fanshawe standing at the rear of the property deeply engaged in studying a large sheet of paper in his hands.

'Good morning, Mr Fanshawe,' said Ravenscroft. 'I would be glad of a few minutes of your valuable time.'

'Morning to you Ravenscroft,' replied Fanshawe folding up the piece of paper. 'If it is about those Moncriefs I don't have the time.'

'No it is not about the Moncriefs. Although, did you know that their real name was Williamson?'

'No, I did not, but I would not be surprised. People like that get through names.'

'I would like a word with you about Claremont.'

'Claremont?' said the builder, surprised.

'Yes, Miss Fincher's home.'

'I know the name of her house,' snapped Fanshawe.

'Of course,' smiled Ravenscroft. 'I understand that you were interested in purchasing the property.'

'I might have been. That was a confidential matter between Miss Fincher and me. It is of no concern of yours.'

'Then you admit that you were anxious to buy the house?'

'As I said, that was a confidential matter between me and Miss Fincher. Now if you don't mind I have to get on and instruct my workmen in the building of this house.'

'May I remind you that two people are dead, both Miss Fincher and her cousin, or rather the man who was pretending to be her cousin, and I need answers to my questions if we are to apprehend the culprit,' said Ravenscroft firmly.

'I suppose you have your work to carry out,' said Fanshawe grudgingly. 'If you must know, yes, I did express an interest in purchasing Claremont. It is a fine building, although a bit neglected, but when Miss Fincher told me that she was not interested in selling, that was an end to the matter.'

'Miss Fincher's maid says otherwise. She has told us that you made three visits to Miss Fincher to push for a sale. That sounds like persistence to me.'

'The maid is mistaken. I only made the one visit. When Miss Fincher said she did not wish to sell Claremont, I accepted her answer.'

'So you would deny that you used the Moncriefs to frighten the old woman.'

'Nonsense. How could I have done that?' retorted Fanshawe.

'Why, by asking them to use Silas Crabbit to scare her to death.'

'What utter piffle,' laughed Fanshawe.

'Is it?'

'Off course it is, Inspector! You and I both know that this Silas Crabbit does not exist, and that he has never existed,' said Fanshawe, raising his voice. 'I did not use any means to frighten or scare Miss Fincher into making her sell Claremont against her will, and that's an end to it.'

'So why did you make the offer in the first place?' persisted Ravenscroft.

'What is that to do with you?

'As I said a few moments ago, this is a police matter. I will repeat my question, Mr Fanshawe, why do you want to buy Claremont?'

Fanshawe let out a loud laugh.

'I do not see what is so funny,' said Ravenscroft.

'Look around you, Inspector. What do you see?'

'I see that you are building this large house.'

'Exactly. I am a builder. I want to buy Claremont so I can knock it down and build a hotel.'

'A hotel?' repeated Ravenscroft.

'Yes. The town is full of schools, boarding houses and hotels, but visitors to Great Malvern often delight in walking on the hills and exploring the nearby villages. That includes Colwall, which I think you will agree is a most attractive village, and with the railway station, a new hotel would prove popular. That is why I wanted Claremont.'

'I would have thought that the site was too small to build a hotel on it.'

'There is some land at the back of it, and I already own the house next door,' explained Fanshawe.

'I see.'

'So if that answers your question, perhaps you will allow me to get on with my work.'

'Certainly Mr Fanshawe, I thank you for your time.'

'See to it that you bring those scoundrels to justice,' shouted the builder as Ravenscroft took his leave.

'You mean the Moncriefs?'

'Of course I mean the Moncriefs!'

Ravenscroft, deep in thought, made his way to the front of the building and retraced his steps down the road in the direction of his horse and trap.

He now knew why Fanshawe had wanted to buy Claremont, but did that mean that the builder had used the Moncriefs and Crabbit to frighten Maud Fincher into selling him the property, and in so doing had bought about the woman's death? But if that had been the case, why would Fanshawe then have killed Rupert Fincher? That did not make sense. Fanshawe would have hoped that he could still have bought the house from him. With Fincher dead, buying Claremont would be more difficult. However there still remained the possibility that Fanshawe had approached Rupert Fincher, unaware that the heir was an imposter, and made him an offer for the property. The two men could then have had a serious disagreement, resulting in the claimant's death — but why would Fanshawe have arranged to meet Fincher in secret by the Swan Pool late in the evening, when the meeting could have taken place in the comfort of the Abbey Hotel?

It did not seem to make any sense — but then, Ravenscroft concluded, stranger things had happened in the past.

CHAPTER TWELVE

SATURDAY

'Nothing, sir,' said Crabb as he sat at the Ravenscrofts' breakfast table on the following morning. 'I went back for nearly ten years and there was no mention of a Silas Crabbit. In fact there were hardly any news stories concerning Ombersley at all, only reports of the annual flower show and other church events. It seems to be one of those sleepy Worcestershire villages where nothing appears to happen from one year to the next.'

'Well, thank you for trying. I have no doubt that you did your best,' said Ravenscroft.

'Do have another piece of toast, Tom,' said Lucy.

'Thank you, Mrs Ravenscroft, I don't mind if I do,' replied Crabb. 'I shall miss these breakfast meetings.'

'Yes, from Monday you will have to answer to Bracket, but I hope that will not be the end of our association,' said Ravenscroft with a little sadness in his voice.

'You and your family will be more than welcome here anytime,' said Lucy, smiling as she poured out some more tea from the pot.

'You are most kind, Mrs Ravenscroft.'

'It would appear that Silas Crabbit was just a name the Moncriefs invented,' said Crabb, buttering his piece of toast, before helping himself to the orange marmalade.

'It would seem that way, but if Silas Crabbit did live in Ombersley and he led an uneventful and lowly existence, it would have been unlikely that his demise would have been reported in the local county newspapers,' said Ravenscroft.

'Many people live and die without leaving any trace behind them,' remarked Lucy.

'Which brings us back to Mr Fanshawe and Marcus Snaith as our main suspects,' said Ravenscroft, cleaning his spectacles vigorously on his napkin.

'Your Mr Snaith seems quite a disreputable character,' said Lucy. 'Getting his poor nephew to impersonate Rupert Fincher so he could acquire Maud Fincher's fortune.'

'I doubt that it was a fortune, although it is sometimes surprising to learn what some people have squirreled away. If Snaith and Pendleton did bring about Maud Fincher's death, and then the solicitor killed the imposter, what could he have expected to gain from it? Without a claimant the estate becomes frozen in the Courts.'

'Then it must be Mr Fanshawe. Some people will stop at nothing to get what they want,' suggested Lucy.

'Yes. But would he really kill two people just so he could acquire Claremont and build a hotel on the site?' answered Ravenscroft. 'And killing the second victim has made the sale less likely.'

'Would visitors really want to stay in a hotel in a village like Colwall?' asked Lucy.

'I don't see why not. It is a very attractive village, with a train station running through it and direct trains to both Birmingham and London, and with easy access to the hills. I think if I didn't know the place I might even go there myself for a holiday,' said Ravenscroft.

'What about your Doctor Cranbrook? You have not mentioned him as one of your main suspects,' remarked Lucy.

'The man is certainly nervous to the point of almost being unwell. You saw, Tom, how his hand shook when we were at the Swan Pool.'

'Doctors often take their own medicines,' added Crabb.

'That is true, but although he was present after the two deaths, and certainly had the opportunity to have killed either, or both, Miss Fincher and Adam Pendleton, I cannot see any reason why he would have done so. He does not stand to benefit from either death.'

'So what do we do now, sir?' asked Crabb.

'I still think the only possible line of investigation that lies open to us is to find out more about Silas Crabbit. I still feel that the Moncriefs might be behind all of this. I know that the newspapers did not mention Crabbit, and that the Moncriefs might have made up the whole thing, but until we have visited Ombersley we will not know one way or the other. When you have finished up your breakfast, Tom, we will fetch the horse and trap and travel over there.'

'It is a frightful day,' said Lucy. 'It is as black as anything and it looks as though there will be heavy rain, so make sure you are suitably attired.'

'Yes, my dear. It will take us an hour or two to get to Ombersley. The place does not have a train station. We may be late back,' said Ravenscroft rising from the table.

'Take care, both of you,' said Lucy.

'Of course. I am not likely to do anything silly two days before I am due to retire.'

* * *

Later that morning, Ravenscroft and Crabb found themselves approaching the picturesque Worcestershire village of Ombersley.

'Here at last,' said Ravenscroft. 'I shall be glad to get out of this pouring rain.'

'Indeed,' answered Crabb, bringing the horse to a slower pace.

'We must have had more rain today than we see in a month. I only hope our visit is worth the effort.'

After passing by a large hotel and coaching inn, they drove down a narrow street, with black-and-white half-timbered buildings on either side. In the distance, a number of chestnut trees stood in front of a tall spired church.

'Let us stop here,' instructed Ravenscroft.

'Where shall we start, sir?' asked Crabb, after he had secured a dry stable for the horse at the local coaching inn.

'Let us find the local post office. They should be able to tell us whether anyone of the name of Crabbit resided in the village,' answered Ravenscroft.

'Is that it over there?'

'"Arthur Bringwood, Grocer and Provisions, Post Office, Wines and Fine Jellies." That should be our starting point.'

Crabb pushed open the old door and the two detectives were soon standing in a small room, with overflowing shelves all around them, and a large counter at the far end.

'Good morning, if you can call it such,' said a small grey-haired man, appearing from an inner room.

'It is indeed a dreadful day,' remarked Ravenscroft, unpleasantly aware of how wet he was from the rain.

'How can I be of assistance to you two gentlemen? You are not from around these parts I would guess.'

'You guess correctly. We have travelled here from Ledbury.'

'Then your journey must have been of an urgent nature to have caused you to venture out on such an inclement day as this.'

'We require some information from you,' began Ravenscroft. 'We are making police enquiries into a Mr Silas Crabbit. This is the post office I presume?'

'It is indeed. Silas Crabbit, you say? I cannot immediately recall the name, although it does seem familiar. Let me look in my book.'

'Thank you, Mr Bringwood.'

Ravenscroft and Crabb waited patiently as the postmaster turned over a number of pages.

'It may have been some years since Mr Crabbit lived here,' suggested Crabb.

'Ah yes, here we are. We have a Mr S. Crabbit at Uphampton, although it does not seem as though we have delivered any post to him there for a number of years.'

'Where is Uphampton?' asked Ravenscroft.

'It is a small hamlet a mile or so from here.'

'And you say that Mr Crabbit has not received any post for some years. When was the last time you delivered post there?'

'I don't know, but my wife may be able to answer your question,' said the postmaster. 'Mildred! Mildred! An enquiry. Come here, if you will!'

'What is it now?' grumbled a stocky, middle-aged woman, entering from the back room.

'Mildred, my dear, these gentlemen are enquiring about Mr Crabbit.'

'Crabbit?'

'Yes, you remember, a Mr S Crabbit, who lives in Uphampton. It seems we have not delivered a letter to him in years.'

'Perhaps you might be able to tell us the last time you delivered any post to Mr Crabbit,' asked Ravenscroft, offering an encouraging smile for the new arrival.

'Why? Who is asking?' asked the woman.

'Detective Inspector Ravenscroft and Sergeant Crabb,' he replied.

'Oh, well, now let me see, it must be four or five years ago,' answered the woman with a scratch of the head.

'Do you happen to know what happened to Mr Crabbit?' asked Crabb.

'What do you mean — what has happened to him? Just because we has not delivered any post to him for years does not mean that anything has happened to him,' retorted Mrs Bringwood. 'Some people don't get any post for years, but it don't mean to say they has left, just that no one has taken the bother to write to them.'

'But something may have happened to him,' persisted Ravenscroft.

The postmaster and his wife looked at each other.

'Did he move away from the area? Did he leave a forwarding address?' asked Ravenscroft.

'No, I don't think so. There is nothing here,' said Bringwood, looking down at his book once more.

'So you do not know what happened to him?'

'No. We just stopped delivering post there, because there was nothing to deliver,' answered the postmaster with a shake of the head.

'I see. Well you have been most helpful to us. You don't have an exact address for Mr Crabbit I suppose?'

'There are only a dozen or so cottages in Uphampton — they don't have names. You should find the one you are looking for quite easily. You takes the Holt Fleet road down past the church, then take the old track on the right just past the Dower House, and you should find yourselves there in about a mile or so. Ask anyone there and they should be able to direct you to Crabbit's cottage,' said the postmaster. 'Of course, you could always purchase one of our local maps.'

'That might be a good idea,' said Ravenscroft reaching into his pocket. 'How much is that?'

'Three shiny pence,' replied the postmaster, handing over the item.

'Thank you. Oh, one more thing before we go. Does the name Williamson mean anything to you?'

'Williamson? No, I don't recall the name,' replied Bringwood, looking again at his wife.

'What about Moncrief?' asked Crabb.

'Oh them Moncriefs; they were a funny pair. They were a damned nuisance, and no mistake,' answered Mrs Bringwood.

'Could you elaborate?'

'They were only here for about three months, about three years ago it was. Always giving themselves airs, they were.' The postmistress became more animated. 'They kept telling us that my mother wanted to get in touch with me, and her being dead for the past thirty years. I gave them short shift, I can tell you.'

'So they were not popular in the village?' prompted Ravenscroft.

'They were not. They might have fooled one or two people with their fancy arty ways, but I saw right through them. In the end I told them not to come into my shop any more. I didn't want folk like that around here. Saying they could speak with the dead,' continued the woman. 'It's against our religion, isn't it?'

'There, there now, Mildred, don't get yourself all worked up. You know that too much excitement is bad for your nerves, so the doctor says.'

'If you want to know all about them Moncriefs, you should ask old Mother Shrewsbury,' said Mrs Bringwood.

'Mother Shrewsbury?' asked Ravenscroft.

'Them Moncriefs took nearly all her savings, they did.'

'Can you tell me where I might find Mrs Shrewsbury's house?'

'You is practically looking at it. It's that cottage, number 2, on the other side of the street.'

* * *

'You were right, sir. Silas Crabbit was a real person and he lived in this Uphampton place,' said Crabb, as he and Ravenscroft closed the door of the post office behind them.

'Before we journey to Uphampton, I think we should pay a call on this Mrs Shrewsbury. She seems to have had a bad experience concerning the Moncriefs.'

The two detectives crossed over the street. Number 2 was a neat half-timbered building, with flowers growing up either side of the door, and late-flowering daffodils in the front garden.

Ravenscroft tapped on the door and was presently rewarded when it was opened by an elderly, grey-haired woman.

'Mrs Shrewsbury?' enquired the detective.

'Yes,' replied the woman.

'My name is Detective Inspector Ravenscroft and this is my colleague, Detective Sergeant Crabb. I would be obliged if we could have a few moments of your time Mrs Shrewsbury,' said Ravenscroft removing his hat.

'Oh, my dears, you looked absolutely drenched! What a day to be out. Hurry yourselves inside.'

'That is most kind of you.'

'Come into the parlour. I've a fire in there. You can dry yourselves out,' said the woman leading the way into a welcoming room, adorned with striped wallpaper, a floral mat, and numerous Staffordshire figurines on the mantelpiece above a blazing fire.

'What a lovely rom,' remarked Crabb.

'Now you just stand over there and dry yourselves before that fire. Have you gentlemen come far? I don't get many visitors these days,' said Mrs Shrewsbury, removing a ball of wool and a newspaper from one of the chairs.

'From Ledbury,' answered Ravenscroft, rubbing his hands in front of the fire.

'My word, you have come a long way. Now while you are drying yourselves out perhaps you would not say no to a warm cup of hot nourishing tea.'

'That is most generous, and welcoming,' smiled Ravenscroft.

'I shan't be a minute. Now, where did I put my spectacles?'

'Perhaps these are them,' said Crabb, picking a pair up from a small side table.

'Oh, thank you, Sergeant. I am always mislaying them. It comes of being old. You are inclined to forget the most simple of things.'

'It happens to us all,' said Ravenscroft.

'Yes, but you are not the same age as I am. Would you say I look eighty-one?'

'I would have said sixty-three,' said Crabb trying to be diplomatic.

'I knew you looked a nice young man. Dear me, now what was I going to do? Oh yes, make the tea. I will be back in a minute or two. Do make yourselves at home.'

'What a delightful lady,' whispered Crabb as the old woman left the room.

'Indeed, and this is such a homely room.'

A few minutes later, Mrs Shrewsbury brought in a silver tray, on which rested three cups of steaming tea and a plate containing pieces of fruitcake.

'Now you drink that, Sergeant,' said Mrs Shrewsbury, handing a cup to Crabb. 'And that one is for you, Inspector, er . . . Now what did you say your name was?'

'Ravenscroft.'

'Well do take a seat, Inspector Ravenscroft, and you as well, young man.'

'Thank you,' said Ravenscroft, taking the chair nearest the fireplace.

'This is most welcoming,' added Crabb.

'Perhaps you would both like to try a piece of my home-made fruitcake. The recipe has been handed down in our family through several generations.'

'This is most delicious,' said Ravenscroft after he had eaten a mouthful.

'I am glad you like it. My grandmother would have been so pleased. Now, how can I be of assistance? You said you had travelled here from Ludlow. It is such a delightful town, really nice buildings, and that wonderful church and old castle on the top of the hill. I went there about twenty years ago, I think.'

'We are from Ledbury,' corrected Ravenscroft. 'Have you ever visited Ledbury?'

'I don't recall having done so. It is somewhere the other side of the Malvern Hills, if I am not mistaken.'

'That is correct. We are here to ask you about Professor Moncrief and his wife, Janet. I believe you knew them quite well when they were living here two or three years ago?' said Ravenscroft before swallowing another mouthful of the welcoming tea.

'Yes, but how do you know I am connected to them?'

'Mr Bringwood, the postmaster over the way, mentioned the matter to us just now.'

'Oh yes, and you are correct, Inspector, when you talk of Janet and the Professor. I knew them quite well.'

'Forgive the intrusion, but I could not help noticing the photograph of the young man in soldier's uniform, on your mantelpiece,' said Ravenscroft.

'Yes that is my late son, Edward. That photograph was taken just before he went to India. He looks so splendid there, does he not, in his new uniform? I was so very proud of him. A few months after he left I received a letter from his commanding officer to say that poor Edward had died there in that foreign land. He had only been in the country for three weeks. He was just twenty-three at the time. It was the fever.' Mrs Shrewsbury's voice was tinged with sadness.

'I am so very sorry,' sympathised Ravenscroft.

'He had his whole life in front of him. He was such a good happy boy. It has been over thirty years now,' said the old woman looking vacantly down at the floor.

'This country has lost a great number of fine men over the years in the cause of Empire. It is a proud legacy,' said Ravenscroft.

'It is nice of you to say so, Inspector. There is hardly a day goes by when I do not look up at that photograph and think of my dear Edward. As the years have gone by I have grown older, but Edward has still remained the same age as he always was. That is a consolation, I suppose.'

'I am sorry to ask you this, but did the Moncriefs say that they could help you in any way to make contact with your son?' asked Ravenscroft tentatively, not wishing to add to the old woman's distress.

'Yes. I remember they held a meeting in the village hall, shortly after they arrived here, saying that they were spiritualists and that they wanted to reunite people with their loved ones. I was so taken by what they were saying that I invited them into my home. We sat round that table over there, and Janet went into a kind of trance, and then she spoke in this strange voice.'

'Silas Crabbit,' ventured Crabb.

'Yes, it was Silas Crabbit. But how do you know about him?' asked Mrs Shrewsbury.

'We have been investigating this couple in Malvern,' answered Ravenscroft. 'But do please go on with your account, if you will.'

'Well, Mr Crabbit said he had spoken with Edward. Of course, at first I did not believe any of this, but he seemed to know certain things about my son that only I knew to be true. I thought it was so wonderful to speak with Edward again after all these years. Janet, or rather Silas, told me that I was not to worry, that Edward was happy and content in his new plane of existence, and that he had watched over me for all of these years. The Professor and Janet seemed such a lovely couple. The Professor was so charming and Janet had such a lovely smile. Then they told me that their dream in life had been to build a church for their religion, where people who wanted to be close to their departed loved ones could go and sit quietly and worship. Later they said that a piece of land had suddenly become vacant in Worcester, where they wanted to build their church, but that they had been unable to commence the building work because they lacked the necessary funds.'

'So then they used Silas Crabbit as a means to acquire the money,' suggested Ravenscroft.

'Yes, but how do you know that?'

'A similar situation involving the Moncriefs has recently occurred in the village of Colwall.'

'I see. Well, Inspector you are correct. I told Janet and the Professor that I had only limited savings, and that I could not help them, but then Silas Crabbit said that Edward was angry with me for not assisting them. When I still refused, Silas turned quite unpleasant.'

'Did Crabbit threaten you in anyway?' asked Crabb, leaning forward in his chair.

'Not exactly, but it was an unhappy time for everyone concerned, so in the end I gave them some money.'

'Could you tell me how much money you gave to the Moncriefs?' asked Ravenscroft, concerned.

'Two hundred pounds. It was nearly all of my savings. They were overjoyed. Mr Crabbit said that Edward had told him that I had done the right thing, that I was not to worry, and that they could now begin building their church and more souls would be saved from despair.'

'What happened afterwards?'

'Nothing. Shortly afterwards, I learned that the Professor and Janet had left Ombersley quite suddenly, leaving no forwarding address. It was all so worrying and disappointing. I have heard nothing from them since, and there has not been any news about the church. It seems that I have been a very foolish woman. I realise now that what they had told me had been only a means to get me to give them money. How could they have been like that, Inspector? All that they told me about Edward was a lie, a terrible lie,' said Mrs Shrewsbury, tears beginning to form in her eyes.

'There, now,' said Ravenscroft sympathetically, 'if it is any consolation you are not the only person that this couple have deceived. We have reason to believe that they played on the fears of an old woman in Colwall.'

'So I am not the only one who was taken in by them?'

'No, we believe that there have been many others,' said Ravenscroft.

'How can they have been so cruel and unfeeling?' asked Mrs Shrewsbury.

'I am afraid that there are some people like that,' said Crabb.

'I must write to this other poor woman in Colwall. She will be need of some assistance and reassurance.'

'I am afraid you cannot do that, Mrs Shrewsbury. The poor woman to whom you refer is unfortunately dead,' said Ravenscroft, lowering his voice.

'Oh dear.'

'We believe that the Moncriefs were attempting to use Silas Crabbit to extract money from this woman. When she refused, they made Crabbit become threatening, and we believe that this distress contributed to the woman's demise.'

'How terrible.'

'What you have told us today has been of great value to us. We have thought for some time that the Moncriefs were only interested in acquiring money from innocent people, such as you. You can rest assured that we will now be able to bring them to account. You say you gave them two hundred pounds? May I be so impertinent as to enquire how you are now able to care for yourself?' asked Ravenscroft, realising that he was asking a delicate question.

'Fortunately I have a small family annuity, which is more than enough for my humble needs,' smiled Mrs Shrewsbury.

'That must be a relief,' said Crabb.

'Had you ever heard of this Silas Crabbit, before the Moncriefs claimed him as their contact with the spirit world?' asked Ravenscroft.

'No, I don't believe that I had heard the name before the séances began.'

'We have been told by Mr Bringwood that a fellow called Crabbit once resided in the nearby hamlet of Uphampton.'

'The first time I heard the name was through Janet Moncrief.'

'If we are able to bring the Moncriefs to justice, would you be prepared to go to court and testify against them?' asked Ravenscroft.

'Oh dear, I don't think I could do that. I don't think I could stand the strain of going through such an ordeal at my age.'

'I quite understand.'

'You see, they did not take the money from me. I gave it to them, of my own free will, because I thought it was the right thing to do. I thought it was what Edward would have wanted. You understand that, don't you, Inspector?'

'Of course.' The detective got to his feet. 'Mrs Shrewsbury, you have been most kind to us.'

'Oh, why don't you stay for another cup of tea?'

'Much as we would like to remain in this pleasant room in the presence of such delightful company for the rest of the day, I am afraid that duty calls. We are on urgent business today.'

'Then it would be unkind of me to delay you any further,' smiled the old woman.

'Thank you for the tea and fruitcake, Mrs Shrewsbury,' said Crabb.

'That is quite alright, Sergeant. You would be most welcome here any time you are passing, and that goes for you as well, Inspector Ravenscroft.'

'You are most kind,' said Ravenscroft, as they made their way out of the parlour.

'When you see next see Janet Moncrief, tell her that I will pray that she will be able to turn her back on her deceitful ways,' said Mrs Shrewsbury, opening the door.

'I will,' said Ravenscroft. 'Good day to you, Mrs Shrewsbury.'

* * *

'Those scoundrels!' said Crabb angrily. He urged the horse past the church and along the narrow rutted lane towards Uphampton. 'Cheating a poor woman like that out of her lifetime savings; it is despicable.'

'Yes it as we thought, the Moncriefs make a living by preying on vulnerable people and extracting money from them, claiming that Silas Crabbit is in touch with their loved ones. They did it with Mrs Shrewsbury. I have no doubt that they did it with Maud Fincher, thereby causing her death, and they are now trying the same thing with Colonel Mortimer and the old ladies of Colwall,' said Ravenscroft.

'I don't know how they can live with themselves.'

'The problem is, will any of their victims come forward to testify against them? We could not put poor Mrs Shrewsbury through the ordeal of a trial. It would be cruel and distressing for her. Then Sefton Rawlinson or some other barrister out to make a name for himself would claim that their victims gave them the money voluntarily and that his clients would have no case to answer.'

'So we have to let those wretched people go free to cause yet more harm?' said Crabb.

'Not at all. The money was given for a purpose, to build a church — and no church has been built. It is a clear case of fraud. I believe we now have enough evidence to bring against them. However we can leave questioning them until tomorrow. The Moncriefs must have known about Crabbit when they were living in Ombersley, and they decided to use him as their spirit guide. The question is — was Crabbit already dead when the Moncriefs arrived here, or did they bring about his death in some way?'

'I suppose he could still be alive.'

'There is only one way to find out — onwards to Uphampton!'

As the two detectives entered the settlement, they observed an old man standing in the porch of one of the cottages.

'Good morning to you,' called out Ravenscroft.

'What's good about it?' grumbled the fellow.

'Yes I am inclined to agree with you. There is too much rain for our liking,' replied Ravenscroft light-heartedly.

'So ye be the cause of it then?'

'I hope not. We require some information.'

'Do you? Well, information costs money.'

'Cheeky fellow,' muttered Crabb.

'You mind your language, young one,' retaliated the man.

'We are looking for Silas Crabbit. I understand he lives around here,' said Ravenscroft, ignoring the last comment.

'Ain't we all looking for Silas? If you can tell me where he's gone to, you will be a better man than me,' replied the fellow, before spitting on the ground and turning abruptly away.

'Wait!' called out Ravenscroft. 'Here is a threepenny piece if you give us the information we require.'

'Who are you, then?'

'Police,' replied Ravenscroft.

'Since when has the police paid anything to anyone?'

'I'm paying now if you give me the answers we are looking for,' said Ravenscroft, holding up the coin. 'When did you last see Silas Crabbit?'

'Be about four years ago.'

'Go on,' urged Ravenscroft.

'Well, he was here one day, and gone the next, and no one has seen head nor tail of him since.'

'Did he say where he was going?' asked Crabb, leaning forward in the trap.

'No. He just left. I saw him on the Sunday, and that was it. He were gone by the Monday.'

'Did anyone think to investigate his absence?' asked Ravenscroft.

'No.'

'Why ever not?'

'Why should we? Folks like to be left alone in these parts. If they decide to go off then it's their business and that's that,' replied the man before again spitting on the ground.

'And he never returned?'

'Not as far as I know.'

'Did Silas Crabbit have any relations, a wife or children perhaps?'

'No, Silas lived alone. He was a miserable, grumpy old devil. No one would have him,' chuckled the old man.

'So he was not well liked in the village?'

'You could say that. We just left him alone, and he left us alone.'

'Where did he live?' asked Ravenscroft.

'That old rickety cottage on the left down there,' indicated the man, pointing.

'Did anyone think to go into the cottage to see if he was still there?' enquired Crabb.

'I suppose we might have done, but then perhaps we didn't. You means he might have died of a bad dream and be still in there?'

'Yes, he could have died in his sleep,' suggested Ravenscroft.

'No, there was no sign of him.'

'Have you ever heard of anyone called Moncrief?'

'Moncrief? No, can't say as I have.'

'They might have visited Silas shortly before he disappeared?' suggested Ravenscroft.

'No, Silas was not one to have visitors.'

'Well, thank you, my man,' said Ravenscroft, handing over the coin.

'Happy to have been of service,' replied the old man, quickly pocketing the coin before turning towards his cottage.

Crabb urged the horse forwards, before pulling up outside a small insignificant looking cottage, where weeds and brambles covered the front garden.

'It seems rather neglected,' remarked Crabb.

'I suppose no one has looked after it for the past four years. Tie the horse to the gate, Tom,' instructed Ravenscroft.

The two men alighted from their trap and pushed their way through the undergrowth until they reached an old wooden door.

'Still open,' said Crabb after raising the latch. 'It's a bit stiff.'

Ravenscroft and Crabb pushed open the door and stepped into a cold dingy room.

'Rather on the smelly side,' remarked Crabb.

'The place has not seen the light of day for several years,' said Ravenscroft looking around the simple room, where the only furniture appeared to be a table, a single chair, a small cupboard and a bed. 'The cobwebs have been the only inhabitants since Crabbit left.'

'At least he's not dead in that bed,' said Crabb, looking down at the crumpled blanket that lay on an almost threadbare mattress.

'Perhaps he spent his whole life in this one-bedroomed place,' said Ravenscroft. 'Have a look in that cupboard and see what you can find.'

'Nothing much here,' said Crabb after he had opened the drawer. 'Just a few worn, dirty clothes. They smell quite a bit.'

'So he obviously did not take all his clothes with him when he left.'

'He could have walked out in his Sunday best.'

'Do people who live like this have a Sunday best?' said Ravenscroft. 'At least it looks as though our Mr Crabbit was able to read. There are two books lying on this table — a worn old Bible and Butcher's *Guide to the Antiquities and Curiosities of Worcestershire*.'

'Get away, you creature!' exclaimed Crabb as a mouse ran over his foot and scuttled out of the front door. 'How did that thing get in here?'

'It must have come in through that hole in the corner. It obviously found it warmer in here than in all that damp and rain outside.'

'Nasty things. We used to have them in the barns when I was growing up on the farm.'

'Well, this is a mystery, Tom. A man walks out of his home one morning, apparently taking nothing with him, and telling no one where he is going, leaving all his clothes behind, but then he seems to disappear off the face of the earth. I think our Mr Crabbit was fully intending to return to this cottage, perhaps later that same day, but then something happened to him to prevent him from doing so.'

'You think he met with an accident of some kind and was left for dead in some ditch?' asked Crabb.

'Possibly, but then surely someone would have found the body. Instead, his neighbour does not report him missing, there is no report in the local newspaper, and he no longer receives any post. Where the devil can he have gone?'

'At least we know that he was a real person.'

'Yes, but how did the Moncriefs learn about him? And why choose him as their spirit guide? We know they were living down the road in Ombersley a year or so later. Had they heard about Crabbit's disappearance from someone, and then decided to use him?'

'I suppose there is nothing for it but to return home,' suggested Crabb.

'You're right, Tom, there is nothing for us here,' said Ravenscroft gloomily, picking up the Bible and shaking the book by its spine. 'No hidden bits of paper here. Butcher's *Guide to the Antiquities and Curiosities of Worcestershire* — that is a strange choice for a man who lived in this house.'

'I am surprised he could read at all,' said Crabb.

'I wonder . . .' Ravenscroft thumbed through the contents of the volume. 'There are no pieces of paper in here, none of the pages have the corners turned down, and yet — what is this? See here, on this page the sentences have all been underlined. Why did he do this?'

'It could have been the previous owner of the book,' suggested Crabb.

'Maybe. Listen to what he has underlined:

> 'Missing Treasure Buried in Boreley Woods.
>
> 'There is an old legend that a Saxon warrior returning home from his campaigns in the north of the country decided to bury a number of coins and other valuables in a secret place inside the great cave in Boreley Woods, meaning to return one day and retrieve his hoard, but failing to do so on account of his early demise. Since then, the treasure has remained hidden. However, the author states that this story is little more than a rumour, passed down by word of mouth through several generations. This story is similar to other reported burial sites at . . .

'And so it goes on.'

'You don't believe any of that nonsense do you?' asked Crabb when Ravenscroft had laid the volume back down on the table.

'History is full of these strange fancies, but although you and I might disregard this article as a work of fiction, Crabbit obviously attached great importance to the story. Where is this Boreley? I thought I saw a fingerpost with the name on it as we were coming here.'

'Shall we look at the map that Mr Bringwood sold us?' suggested Crabb.

'Of course.' Ravenscroft retrieved the map from his inside coat pocket and spread it out on the table.

'There it is,' said Crabb.

'About a mile or so from here, as the crow flies. If we carry on up this road, then take this track off to the left we should then reach the woods. It appears to be quite near the River Severn,' said Ravenscroft tracing the route with his finger.

'You think Crabbit went out one day to find that treasure?' asked Crabb.

'It is a likely possibility. Perhaps that is why he never came back. He acquired this old book from somewhere, read this page, and went out looking for treasure,' said Ravenscroft, thinking out loud.

'It all sounds very fanciful.'

'It is all that we have to go on. I know it is a bad day, but now we have come this far, it would be a pity if we did not try to follow the route that Crabbit may have taken. Let us see if we can find these woods and the cave that the book mentions.'

Ravenscroft and Crabb closed the door of the cottage behind them and made their back to the trap.

* * *

A few minutes later Crabb drew up the horse on the edge of a large wood.

'Tie the horse up there, Tom. The wood is too dense to take a horse and trap through it, so we will have to go forward on foot,' said Ravenscroft, turning the collar of his coat up against the elements.

'This looks like it might once have been a path,' said Crabb.

The two men entered the wood and followed the way into the interior. After a few minutes had elapsed, the path ended suddenly in a small clearing.

'Which way now?' asked Crabb, looking all around him.

'Perhaps over there. The undergrowth is less dense there, so people may have used that way in the past,' answered Ravenscroft.

The two men pushed forwards, until another path gradually started to appear.

'It looks as though we chose the right way,' said Ravenscroft.

'It could lead to the cave mentioned in the book.'

The two detectives ducked the overhanging branches and proceeded deeper into the wood.

'Look there!' suddenly exclaimed Ravenscroft. 'I think we might have reached our destination.' He peered across at the entrance to a large cave.

'The rock surface seems to go up a long way.'

'Well, Tom, let's take a look inside, and see what we can find. It looks as though some quarrying may have taken place here long ago.'

Ravenscroft stepped carefully over the fallen pieces of rock that littered the cave's entrance. 'It appears to go back some way, and the floor is covered in water, to a depth of several inches. It is caused by all this rain, no doubt.'

'It will be getting quite dark inside soon,' remarked Crabb, following his superior further into the cave.

'Duck down here!' called out Ravenscroft, leading the way. 'The roof of the cave is getting lower. We seem to be going downwards. We should still be able to see for another few hundred yards or so, as long as this rising water does not make it too difficult to proceed.'

'It is a pity we did not bring the carriage lamp with us,' said Crabb.

'But when we left home today we never thought we would be exploring a cave in the middle of a wood in wild Worcestershire. It is getting very wet and overbearing in here. I cannot see the point in going on. If either Crabbit's remains or the buried treasure are in this cave, they are both completely inaccessible due to the depth of the water.'

'The water must be coming down the walls of the cave, due to the wet ground all around it.'

'Let's get out of here. What's that?' called out Ravenscroft.

'It sounds as though some of the rock is about to give way!'

'Quickly, Tom, get out!'

'The rocks are coming down!' cried out Crabb, as the two men were suddenly violently flung up against the side of the cave.

After the fall, there was only silence.

CHAPTER THIRTEEN

The interior of the cave filled with the rising, choking dust from the fallen rock. Then a suffocating, eerie darkness descended.

'Sir! Sir!' called out Crabb.

'Over here, Tom,' answered Ravenscroft faintly in the darkness. 'Are you alright?'

'I think so,' replied Crabb, brushing the loose pieces of debris from his hair and jacket. 'How are you, sir?'

'I think I am still in one piece. That was a mighty fall,' said Ravenscroft coughing.

'I can't see a thing.'

'Don't move at all. Our eyes must adjust to this darkness. We may be able to find a way out in a minute or so, but until then it is safer to remain perfectly still. The last thing we want to do is to disturb any more of the loose rock above us,' said Ravenscroft, coughing again in an attempt to clear the dust from his chest and throat.

The two men remained silent as they listened to the sound of dripping water.

'I think everything is still. I can just about make out where the rock fell,' said Ravenscroft reaching for his spectacles so that he could remove the dust from them. 'Damn, one of my spectacle lenses is broken. Can you see anything, Tom? I think you are nearer to the entrance.'

'It looks as though there has been quite a large rock fall.'

'Let me see. I think I can make my way over there,' said Ravenscroft, replacing his spectacles and making his way slowly across the cave. 'Good grief! You're right, Tom; it looks as though our way out is completely blocked.'

'We could try to move some of these rocks,' said Crabb, bending down.

'No!' called out Ravenscroft. 'If we move any of them it may cause the rest to come down on top of us.'

'Perhaps if we went further into the cave there might be another way out?' suggested Crabb.

'You could be right. If I strain my eyes, I think I can see a small chink of light in the distance,' said Ravenscroft pointing ahead of him. 'Can you see it?

'I think so. Yes, yes, I can see that it is definitely lighter ahead of us.'

'Then we should move slowly towards that and pray that we may yet find another way out of these caves. Let me go first.'

Ravenscroft inched his way between the walls of the cave, as Crabb followed carefully behind.

'Watch your head again!' said Ravenscroft stooping down. 'Yes, it is certainly lighter ahead.'

'The water does not seem so deep here,' said Crabb, looking down at his wet boots.

'My God, what's that?' called out Ravenscroft. 'Look down there, Tom!'

Crabb inched forwards in the gloom.

'It looks like a skeleton. Good Lord, it must be the remains of Silas Crabbit. He must have come into these caves and met with some kind of accident and died here,' said Ravenscroft.

'But surely if he came in the same way as we did, he would have got out the same way,' suggested Crabb.

'Not if he never regained consciousness.'

'How awful!'

'He could have slipped and hit his head, or perhaps he was caught in a rock fall. If he was badly injured then his only hope of survival was to wait, in the hope that someone would come looking for him, but then, of course, no one did.'

'The poor man. It does not bear thinking about. To die all alone in this horrible cave,' said Crabb.

'Well at least we know what happened to Silas Crabbit. There is nothing we can do for him now. We must think of ourselves. Let's hope that light ahead of us is an indication that there is another exit. There is only one way to find out.'

Ravenscroft and Crabb continued on their journey, getting closer and closer to the ray of daylight ahead of them.

'Look out!' cried out Ravenscroft as a few more pieces of rock fell on to the two men. 'Quickly, we are nearly there.'

Crabb and Ravenscroft walked into the shaft of light and found that they were now standing in a sunlit chamber. The light, however, came from a large hole in the rock far above them.

'It must be thirty or forty yards or more to the top,' said Ravenscroft straining his eyes as he peered upwards.

'There does not seem to be any other out of this chamber,' said Crabb.

'And there is no way either of us can scramble up that wall of rock. Anyway, it looks decidedly unstable. Even if we were Alpine climbers and managed to get a foothold somewhere on the way up, I fear there would be a great risk that the rock wall might still come down on top of us.'

'What can we do now?' asked Crabb, sounding concerned.

'There is nothing we can do. All we can hope is that someone will come looking for us. We cannot go back through the cave, as that way is blocked.'

'But who knows where we are?'

'We told Mrs Ravenscroft that we were going to Ombersley this morning. If we fail to return by tomorrow she will no doubt raise the alarm. All we can hope for is that someone will retrace our steps to that post office in Ombersley, and that the trail will then lead them to Crabbit's cottage, and that they will find the book and realise where we have gone. Alternatively, someone might spot the horse and trap on the edge of the wood and send out a search party.'

'I hope so,' said Crabb, trying to cover the fear in his voice.

'I am sorry, Tom. I should not have entered the cave.'

'There was no way of telling that it was about to fall in on itself.'

'I know, but I should not have taken the risk,' said Ravenscroft, disconsolate. 'I had no right to risk your life as well as my own.'

'Don't worry, sir. I'm sure that someone will come looking for us.'

'Inspector Bracket will be taking over on Monday. When we don't appear I am sure he will raise the alarm. His first case will be to come looking for us,' said Ravenscroft trying to make light of the situation.

'I don't like the look of that rock above us; some of it seems quite loose.'

'If it is any consolation, that rock has been there for thousands of years and there is little debris on the floor of this chamber, so it may be more stable than we think. Then again, with all this rain, it is well sodden. Either way, we cannot get up there. Let us sit on that rock over there, at the side of the chamber. We may have some cover if bits break off and fall.'

The two men sat down on the boulder and again surveyed their surroundings.

'I can't help thinking of poor old Crabbit,' said Crabb. 'He was completely alone down here, with no one even aware of where he had gone.'

'Yes. At least we know that our loved ones will miss us and decide to come looking for us. We must cling to that hope. I am sure that all will be well.'

'I am sure you are right.'

'Do you know what interests me — how did the Moncriefs learn about Crabbit? We know that they lived only a mile or two apart in different villages. Janet Moncrief mentioned a cave. She said that Crabbit was somewhere in a cave. How did they know that Crabbit died here?'

'Perhaps they came looking for him one day and found his remains, just as we did?' suggested Crabb.

'Yes, but why would they have come looking for him?'

'They were after the treasure as well?'

'They certainly didn't find it, otherwise they would not now be trying to extract money from old ladies.'

'Perhaps Crabbit told them what he was going to do?'

'That is highly unlikely. If you were going to search for buried treasure you would not go and tell someone else what you were intending to do. You would want to keep it all to yourself. No, this is all a complete mystery. Janet Moncrief definitely mentioned the cave when she was referring to Crabbit. Why?'

'Maybe they have been in contact with him in the other world?' suggested Crabb.

'I don't know. In situations like this you begin to believe in anything, and everything. I am very sorry to have got you into this situation.'

'That's alright, sir.'

'My life in the force is due to end in two days, whereas you have another thirty years of policing ahead of you.'

'With Inspector Bracket in charge,' Crabb joked.

'Oh, he probably is not such a bad fellow. I'm sure you will get on well with him. See it as your mission in life to point him in the right direction, and anyway I am sure that one day you will become an inspector yourself. Then you, too, will have an assistant to order about, and you will go on to solve many crimes,' replied Ravenscroft as lightly as he could.

'No, Bracket will never be as good as you are, sir.'

'Now, Tom, don't you go singing my praises or I may start to cry, and remember it is me that got you into this mess. You did not deserve that.'

'We have been through some interesting times over the past six years or so,' said Crabb.

'Yes, we certainly have. We have done more than our fair share of bringing various villains to account, and we have certainly found ourselves in some tricky situations over the years. I remember that time we were trapped in that underground room in Upton, then when I went to New York . . . but all that is in the past. We must look forward now to the future. It is not all over yet.'

* * *

'What time is it, sir?' asked Crabb.

'It is just gone past three. We have been down here nearly three hours now.'

'It will be dark in a few hours.'

'The sun has already moved round; there is less daylight in here. At least it appears to have stopped raining.'

'I think you mentioned your sister Anne, and that the Moncriefs claimed to have made contact with her,' said Crabb changing the subject.

'Yes. I never knew her personally, of course. She died shortly after I was born, but while I was growing up it was as if she was always there. Every year on her birthday we would climb the hill to the churchyard to lay flowers on her grave. My parents missed her very much. There was always a place laid at the dinner table for her, as though they were expecting her to open the kitchen door and enter at any moment. I remember my mother saying to me once that I had nothing to fear in this life, as Anne would always be looking out for me, and I suppose in a strange way she always has. In moments of great danger I have always felt her presence. That is why when I went to the Moncriefs' séance and they seemed to know all about Anne, I almost believed in what they were doing. It was not until later that I came to the realisation that I had been deceived. There was no way in which Janet Moncrief could have summoned up Crabbit to say that he had spoken with Anne. What little they knew about her I had inadvertently told them. Then I knew how they had cheated others in a similar way.'

'Do you have any regrets in life?' asked Crabb.

'Regrets? Only two come to mind. I wish I had left London much sooner and come to live in this fine part of the country, where I would have found Mrs Ravenscroft. Conversely, the second regret is that I did not stay in Whitechapel a few months longer and catch Jack the Ripper. By the time that evil man had started his atrocities I had already left. But then again, perhaps that is just vanity. If all my former colleagues were unable to catch him, what right have I to think that I might have done better? What about yourself, Tom? Do you have any regrets?'

'I have none that I can think of. I knew my Jennie when we were both quite young. We lived in the same village and it seemed perfectly natural that we would get married, so I have no regrets about that. I have been very lucky to have had the love of a great woman and to have had three lovely children.'

'Yes, our children are our future, we sometimes forget that,' agreed Ravenscroft. 'No matter what we are able to do in this life, it is our children who will carry the flame forward, as it were. We can only hope that they make a better life for themselves in the future. All we can do is to give them all the support we can.'

'Sorry to interrupt, sir, but I thought I heard something above,' said Crabb.

'It is probably an animal.'

'Help! Help! We're down here!' called out Crabb.

'Hello there?' shouted a voice in reply.

'Thank God,' said Ravenscroft.

'Can you help us? We are trapped down at the bottom,' Crabb shouted back. 'There has been a fall and the cave entrance is blocked.'

'Get a rope!' instructed Ravenscroft. 'You could pull us up.'

The two detectives waited for an answer, but received none.

'Is anyone there?' asked Ravenscroft.

'They could have gone off to get help,' said Crabb.

'Yes, Tom, I am sure you are right. All we can do now is sit here and hope that they return. I am only thankful that they found us.'

* * *

'They are taking their time,' grumbled Crabb after another hour had passed, during which the light in the cave had grown increasingly gloomier.

'If they had to go back to Ombersley and then gather assistance and secure a rope of some sort that would account for the delay, but I am confident that we will not have too much longer to spend in this wretched place.'

'What will we do next, sir, regarding the case?' asked Crabb, trying to fill the silence.

'Once we are out of this cave and we are able to return home, tomorrow we will go and see the Moncriefs. They have a lot to answer for, and I am sure they are the cause of all this mystery. I am pretty sure that they caused Maud Fincher's death. I still do not know why they killed Adam Pendleton, but I intend to find out. Then there is the question of Silas Crabbit. Did they know Crabbit, and what part, if any, did they play in his death? I want this case concluded before I hand over to Bracket on Monday.'

'What's that!' said Crabb, suddenly springing to his feet.

'They appear to be lowering a rope,' answered Ravenscroft. 'Hello there!'

'Tie the rope round you, and we will pull you up,' came a distant cry from somewhere above them.

'Here, tie this rope under your arms,' instructed Ravenscroft, moving quickly out of the way as a piece of loose rock came down the shaft.

'You go first, sir,' replied Crabb.

'No, I insist that you go. I shall be alright until the rope comes back.'

'It is only right that you should go first.'

'Sergeant Crabb, as your superior officer I am ordering you to go first,' insisted Ravenscroft.

'Then it seems that I must obey your order, but with great reluctance.'

'Good man,' said Ravenscroft. He wrapped the rope under Crabb's arms and tied it firmly. 'Use your feet on the side walls to give you some support.'

'I'll try not to dislodge any of the rock on the way up.'

'If anything happens to me, make sure you secure justice for Maud Fincher and Adam Pendleton.'

'You can count on that.'

'We are ready,' shouted out Ravenscroft. 'Lift up!'

'See you on the top,' smiled Crabb.

Ravenscroft looked upwards as Crabb began his slow ascent towards the open air.

'Sorry, sir!' yelled out Crabb as his feet touched the side of the shaft. Debris came hurtling down, narrowly missing Ravenscroft.

'Are you alright, sir?' asked Crabb.

'I am alright, Tom. Keep going! You are nearly there.'

Hands from above reached out for Crabb and he quickly disappeared from view.

'Thank God!' uttered Ravenscroft.

He waited anxiously and then watched as the rope was gradually lowered again. 'Nearly here!'

As Ravenscroft reached out to grasp the rope, he heard a noise above him, and moved quickly out of the way as more pieces of rock tumbled down in his direction. Then he felt a sharp pain as a rock hit him on the temple, sending him sprawling on to the wet floor. He struggled to get to his feet.

'Sir? Sir?' he could hear Crabb call somewhere in the distance. 'Let me go down and get him.'

'No, stay where you are,' answered Ravenscroft as he forced himself to see through the shadows that crossed his eyes. 'I have the rope.'

Ravenscroft passed the rope under his arms and gradually made a knot.

'Ready!' he called out in a distant voice that seemed to him not to be his own.

Ravenscroft felt his feet being lifted off the floor of the chamber. He desperately clung on to the rope.

'We will soon have you up, sir,' called his sergeant.

His feet brushed against the sides of the walls. Yet more rocks fell around him. The rope hurt under his arms as he felt his energy draining away. He closed his eyes again and knew that he could not go on.

Then he heard his mother's voice calling out — 'Anne, Anne.'

'Anne,' he mumbled. 'Is it you?'

'Anne, Anne Ravenscroft,' replied the distant voice.

'Hang on, sir!' yelled Crabb.

Then arms were reaching out for him.

Suddenly the rope slipped away and he fell back down the shaft.

'Again!' yelled Crabb. 'Secure the rope, you men!'

The rope stopped unravelling with a painful jerk. His feet touched the sides once more — and he felt himself being slowly pulled upwards again.

'We've got you,' shouted out Crabb reassuringly, as many hands pulled him securely over the edge.

Ravenscroft breathed heavily, aware of the damp grass beneath him, as he looked up at the sky.

'We only got you out just in time, Ravenscroft. Another few seconds and the whole lot would have caved in on you,' said a familiar voice.

'Bracket!' exclaimed Ravenscroft. 'What the devil are you doing here?'

CHAPTER FOURTEEN

SUNDAY

'Samuel, wake up,' said Lucy.

'Oh I'm sorry, I must have fallen asleep again,' replied Ravenscroft, rubbing his eyes. 'What time is it?'

'Ten o'clock.'

'Then I must get up as soon as possible. Tom will be here at twelve, and then we have to go and see the Moncriefs.'

'You will stay where you are for at least another hour. I have bought you up a cup of beef tea.'

'Thank you, my dear,' said Ravenscroft, raising himself up on to the pillow. 'Oh, my head aches!'

'I'm not surprised. You have a rather large bruise on your forehead.'

'A rock fell on it when I was at the bottom of that damn cave.'

'It seems to me that you and Tom both had a lucky escape. I saw both of you off in the morning fully expecting you to return before nightfall, and instead you led poor Tom into that dreadful cave. Whatever were you thinking?' Lucy reprimanded him lightly. 'I cannot let you out on your own without you getting into trouble. It is a good job all that will cease after tomorrow.'

'Don't remind me. I know. I'm very sorry. I just wanted to find out what had happened to Silas Crabbit, in the hope that I might be able to draw this case to a satisfactory conclusion.'

'And have you?'

'Have what?'

'Drawn this case to a satisfactory conclusion?'

'Not exactly. At least we now know how the Moncriefs get their money: by using Crabbit as a means of frightening their victims. I am sure they must be behind the deaths of Maud Fincher and Adam Pendleton. That is why Tom and I will be interviewing them again this afternoon.'

'It was fortunate that Inspector Bracket was able to rescue you, otherwise you would have still been there now,' said Lucy.

'Yes, I realise that we have had a very lucky escape. Who knows how long the rocks above us would have remained in place before crashing on to us?'

'How did he find you, anyway?'

'It seems that Alphonse Bracket had been following us for several days. He said that he had a few days off before he starts here on Monday and thought it would be valuable opportunity to practice his shadowing skills by tracking Tom and me, without giving himself away,' said Ravenscroft somewhat indignantly. 'The audacity of the man.'

'He seems to have been successful.'

'I did get the feeling once or twice this week that someone was following us.'

'I say it was a good job that he did.'

'Yes. He followed us to Ombersley and then to Crabbit's cottage, and eventually found the trap on the edge of the wood. Then he lost track of our route and had to make several detours until he discovered the upper entrance into the cave. That is why we were there for several hours. He knew we had gone into the wood, but he did not know why we had gone there.'

'I say jolly good for Inspector Bracket,' echoed Lucy.

'Yes, I suppose we owe him our lives.'

'So your successor is not all that bad after all. I am sure that he will make a very good job of solving crimes in the Three Counties.'

'You are probably right. You are usually very intuitive when it comes to these things,' said Ravenscroft, somewhat begrudgingly.

'Now don't be so grumpy.'

'I am not grumpy,' protested Ravenscroft. 'I only want to solve this case before I hand everything over to Bracket.'

'And I am sure that you will. Drink up your tea and rest for another hour. I will come and wake you just before twelve and put something on that bruise before you go out.'

Ravenscroft looked at his wife with affection. 'Whatever would I do without you?'

'Probably get into more danger!' joked Lucy. 'It is a mystery to me how you survived for all those years in London before you met me.'

'Yes, I have sometimes wondered about that as well. Someone must have been watching over me.'

* * *

'So, Tom, are we ready?' asked Ravenscroft later that afternoon as he and Crabb alighted from the trap outside the Moncriefs' house.

'I cannot wait to bring those mountebanks to account,' said Crabb, as he secured the horse.

Ravenscroft reached out and pulled the bell handle.

Professor Moncrief opened the door and smiled when he saw who it was. 'Why, Inspector Ravenscroft, what an unexpected pleasure. What brings you here on such a fine afternoon?'

'We require you to answer some more questions, Professor Moncrief,' said Ravenscroft in a serious tone of voice.

'Who is it, Felix?' called a familiar voice from inside.

'It is Inspector Ravenscroft, my dear. He wants to ask us some more questions. The Inspector sounds very serious.' Moncrief opened the door wider and beckoned the two detectives to enter. 'You had better come in. I think you know the way by now.'

Ravenscroft and Crabb walked into the living room.

'How pleasant to see you again,' said Janet Moncrief. 'Do please take a seat. I quite feared for your safety yesterday. Perhaps I can offer you some refreshment?'

'Thank you; that will not be necessary,' replied Ravenscroft, seating himself at the end of the sofa.

'Now how can we help you?' asked Moncrief.

'We know about Silas Crabbit,' announced Ravenscroft.

'I am sorry, I do not quite understand.'

'We know that when you lived in Ombersley, Crabbit lived in the nearby hamlet of Uphampton. Is that where you met him?'

'I can assure you, Inspector, that we never met Silas when he was alive. The first we knew about Silas was when he contacted Janet from his place in the spirit world.'

'So you deny having ever meeting Silas Crabbit in this life?'

'That is what we have just said,' answered Moncrief.

'Mrs Moncrief, you said a moment ago when we entered the room that you feared for my safety. Can you elaborate further?'

'I know that you have been in a dangerous situation, where you feared for your life, but we always knew that all would be well with you.'

'I think that the bruise on my forehead might have informed you of that fact, but yes, you are correct, Mrs Moncrief, both my sergeant and I did find ourselves in a perilous situation yesterday. Fortunately for us, deliverance was on hand. How did you know about the cave?'

'The cave?' The Professor sounded bewildered.

'When I was here last, Mrs Moncrief told me that Silas Crabbit had said something about a cave.'

'Yes,' she agreed. 'Silas often speaks of the cave.'

'You mean the cave in Boreley Woods?'

'He never tells us where it is situated: only that something frightening happened to him in a cave.'

'Yesterday, we saw the remains of Silas Crabbit.'

'Oh, how terrible!' said Janet Moncrief, shocked.

'He met with a serious accident in the cave four years ago, and died there. Apparently at the time he was looking for buried treasure. Do you know anything about this?'

'No, neither my wife nor I know anything about any buried treasure, nor about the circumstances of poor Silas's death, I can assure you. In a strange way it is rather comforting to learn how he died.'

'The poor man. Now we know how he died, I will be after to offer him some comfort when I next speak with him,' said Janet Moncrief, saddened.

Ravenscroft gave a wry smile. 'While we were in Ombersley we also spoke with a Mrs Shrewsbury. Does the name mean anything to you?'

'Why yes of course. Mrs Shrewsbury was one of our most devout followers. She was a most delightful lady. She was a true believer,' said Professor Moncrief.

'You cheated her out of two hundred pounds,' said Crabb. 'Her life savings.'

'You are misinformed, Sergeant. It is true that Mrs Shrewsbury did make a small donation to our cause,' answered Moncrief.

'I would not say that two hundred pounds was a small donation,' corrected Ravenscroft.

'No, indeed. To some people, two hundred pounds is indeed a large sum of money.'

'Mrs Shrewsbury gave you the money towards the building of your spiritualist church in Worcester, is that not correct?'

'Yes that is indeed so.'

'She claims that since she gave you the money you left Ombersley, and she has never heard from you again.'

'That is not quite true. Janet has written to Mrs Shrewsbury on a number of occasions informing her of our plans, and assuring her that the church is to be built very shortly. The only difference is that now the church will be built in Malvern Link rather than in Worcester, owing to the generosity of Mr Fanshawe,' said Moncrief.

'Mrs Shrewsbury did not mention any such letters,' said Ravenscroft, staring intently at the spiritualist to see whether his persistent line of questioning would cause any break in the other's outward condescending manner.

'I can assure you that Janet has written several such letters. Is that not so, my dear?'

'Yes, of course.'

'Sometimes as we get older, we forget these small things,' Moncrief explained.

'I have to tell you both that I do not believe a word of this. I think you used the voice of Silas Crabbit as a means of frightening the old lady into parting with her money, and that once you secured it, you decided to leave the village and move to Shipston-on-Stour. Intimidating a poor old woman and cheating her out of her savings is a criminal offence,' said Ravenscroft, finding himself becoming more heated.

'As I have just said, Inspector, all of this is a terrible misunderstanding. Mrs Shrewsbury was only too happy to make a donation to our mission. She was a true believer and was anxious to establish our church. I can assure you that no undue influence was placed on the poor lady. Janet will write to her again tomorrow at the earliest opportunity, won't you, my dear?'

'Yes, of course.'

'Does that mean that you will return the money to Mrs Shrewsbury?' asked Crabb.

'Why yes, of course. If Mrs Shrewsbury decides that she wants her donation returned, then we will only be too happy to carry out her wishes. We do not seek to hurt people in this world, Inspector, or to force them to do anything against their will.'

'All very convenient,' remarked Ravenscroft, annoyed. 'Is that what you did to Maud Fincher?'

'What are you implying?' asked Janet Moncrief.

'I believe you used Crabbit as a means of trying to extract money from Maud Fincher. When she was reluctant to agree to your demands, you then made sure that Crabbit became ever more demanding and unpleasant, so much so that Miss Fincher feared for her life, and that all this increased anxiety resulted in her demise.'

'I beg to differ,' said Professor Moncrief. 'That is certainly not what happened. Maud Fincher was one of our most loyal and devoted followers. We would never have pressurised her in that way.'

'Did you ask her for money?' asked Crabb.

'No certainly not. We would never ask our followers to donate to our cause against their will. I admit that we do accept donations, but they are always freely given, and can of course be returned to those who made the donation, should they so wish.'

'What about Colonel Mortimer? Have you taken money from him?' asked Ravenscroft. He was becoming more and more frustrated with the answers he was receiving from the couple.

'That is an entirely confidential matter between the Colonel and ourselves,' replied Professor Moncrief.

'May I remind you, Professor Moncrief, that this is a serious police matter. We are looking into the unexpected deaths of two innocent people. We require an answer — have you taken money from Colonel Mortimer?'

'The good Colonel has made one or two small donations towards our building project, but as I said just now, they were freely given.'

'And have you taken money from Miss Jayward and Mrs Tinniswood?' asked Ravenscroft.

'Both ladies are enthusiastic supporters of our mission, as I think you have witnessed, and they were only too happy to make contributions,' said Felix Moncrief.

'It is extremely unlikely that Mr Fanshawe will be building your church. We have spoken with the said gentleman, and he is far from happy with your activities, I can assure you.'

'Mr Fanshawe is considering our request, despite his scepticism. We look forward to the day when our church is built,' said Janet Moncrief enthusiastically.

'If your church is not built, can we assume that you will be returning all these donations to their rightful owners?'

'Should they wish it, of course we would only be too happy to comply with their desires, but we still live in hope that our church will be built in the near future, and that all the good citizens of Malvern, and those further afield, will be able to experience our mission to the full.'

Ravenscroft was tiring of the couple's intransigence. He decided to alter his line of questioning. 'Why did you kill Adam Pendleton?'

'Who is Adam Pendleton?' asked Professor Moncrief, showing signs of unease.

'He was the man pretending to be Miss Fincher's cousin, Rupert Fincher,' said Crabb.

'We know nothing of this, Inspector. We knew that Maud's cousin was present at the funeral service, but that is all we know.'

The questioning was not going as Ravenscroft had hoped it would. If he was to get a sudden confession from the couple, he would need to be more forthright.

'Well, Professor Moncrief,' he persisted, 'I have to tell you that the man who claimed to be Rupert Fincher was an imposter whose real name was Adam Pendleton. He was brutally murdered next to the Swan Pool in the Priory Gardens. I believe that you killed him because you believed he stood between you and Maud Fincher's estate. You were hoping to lay claim to her inheritance.'

'That is preposterous!' declared Moncrief. 'How could we have claimed his inheritance by carrying out such a despicable act?'

'Rupert Fincher confronted you with what he had discovered regarding your treatment of his cousin, and you retaliated by killing the poor man,' said Ravenscroft, trying to sound convincing, when he knew that he was treading an uncertain path.

'Why would we have done that? You have just admitted to us that this man was an imposter,' retaliated Felix Moncrief.

'Yes, but you did not know this at the time. You thought you were still confronting Maud Fincher's cousin. It will be easier for you both if you confess now.'

'Inspector, I think you are still suffering from the effects of the "perilous situation" you spoke of earlier,' said Moncrief. 'Perhaps it might be better if we resumed this conversation at a later date?'

'I can assure you that I am quite well. I urge you to tell us all you know.'

'But we have told you everything, Inspector. There is nothing more we can add,' said Janet Moncrief. 'We appreciate that you are anxious to solve this case as soon as possible, but really I do not think we can be of any further assistance to you.'

'You are correct, Mrs Moncrief, when you say that we are anxious to secure justice for Adam Pendleton and Maud Fincher. This is not an end of the matter.' Deflated, Ravenscroft rose quickly to his feet. 'In the meantime, I suggest that you send back the money you extracted from Mrs Shrewsbury.'

'As I said earlier, Janet will write to Mrs Shrewsbury, and if she is any way unhappy with what has taken place, we will make sure that her donation is returned,' said Professor Moncrief.

'My sergeant will be paying Mrs Shrewsbury a visit at the end of the week, and if he finds that her money, this so-called donation, has not been returned, then it will become a criminal matter for which you will both have to answer in a court of law,' said Ravenscroft.

'But we cannot be prosecuted for what we have not done,' protested Moncrief. 'All donations to our cause are made purely on a voluntary understanding. There is no criminal intent.'

'You have until the end of the week.'

'Dear Inspector Ravenscroft, I am so sorry to see you so annoyed. I will ask Anne to watch over you, and ease the way ahead,' said Janet Moncrief.

'How dare you speak the name of my dead sister!' shouted Ravenscroft, turning to confront her. 'You have no right to involve my personal life in your wretched affairs!'

'Come, sir,' urged Crabb, placing his hand on Ravenscroft's shoulder. 'You are better than this.'

Ravenscroft glared angrily at the couple, before quickly leaving the room, and slamming the front door behind him and Crabb.

* * *

'Those insufferable people,' snapped Ravenscroft as he and Crabb climbed into the trap. 'Drive away from this wretched place as fast as you can, Tom, before I get out and return to give them another piece of my mind.'

'They seem to have an answer for everything,' sympathised Crabb.

'They are cunning, and totally without scruples. I am damned if I will let them get the better of me.'

'They have no morals.'

'We know that they have cheated all those poor people out of their savings, but instead of admitting it, they give us all this sanctimonious nonsense about people making them donations. We also know from her own letter that they frightened poor Maud Fincher to death, and I am sure they were involved in Adam Pendleton's death. They seem to keep changing their names backwards and forwards each time they move to a new location. But we cannot prove a single accusation against them, and that is the most annoying thing of all.'

'It does not seem right that villains like that can take advantage of poor innocent souls.'

'I am only sorry that you had to witness my unprofessional behaviour towards them when we left. I should not have lost my temper with them. It was unforgivable,' said Ravenscroft.

'That is quite understandable. I would have done the same if it was my sister,' replied Crabb, urging the horse forward.

'But you don't have a sister.'

'I know. But if I did, I would have reacted in the same way.'

'Promise me one thing, Tom.'

'Anything, sir.'

'That you will visit poor Mrs Shrewsbury at the end of the week and make sure that her money is returned.'

'You can depend on that.'

'Good man.' Ravenscroft was calmer now. 'This case is a complete mess, and I am out of time to solve it. There is nothing else for it, I will have to hand everything over to you and Bracket in the morning. I wanted so much to solve this crime, but sadly I have failed.'

'Don't say that. You have made excellent progress. We will keep on gaining evidence against those Moncriefs. I am sure they will give themselves away sooner or later,' answered Crabb reassuringly. 'It is only a matter of time.'

'Do you know, Tom, there was a moment in there when I actually began to doubt my own judgement and intuition?'

'What do you mean, sir?'

'Almost certainly the Moncriefs are charlatans and thieves, and I am positive that they bought about the death of Maud Fincher, but I simply do not see them killing Adam Pendleton.'

'But you said in there that they had an argument with him, and that they killed him as a result.'

'I know, but now I am not so sure. Come to breakfast tomorrow, and then I will formally hand over everything to you and Bracket.'

'Yes, sir — but if, as you say, the Moncriefs did not kill Adam Pendleton, then who did?' asked Crabb.

'I wish I knew, Tom. I wish I knew.'

CHAPTER FIFTEEN

MONDAY

'Good morning, Tom.' Ravenscroft could not hide his sullen mood as he sat down at the breakfast table on the following morning.

'Good morning to you, sir,' replied Crabb, trying to sound as cheerful as he could.

'Would you like some tea, Tom?' asked Lucy.

'Thank you, Mrs Ravenscroft.'

'Well, my final day has come,' announced Ravenscroft.

'And I shall be the sadder for it. I will miss you.'

'It is good of you to say so, Tom.'

'It won't be the same working with Inspector Bracket.'

'Oh I am sure you two will get on well enough. He seems a decent enough fellow.'

'He did save your lives,' added Lucy.

'He did indeed, and I am most grateful for it. After we have eaten breakfast we will go over to the station and wait for your new superior's arrival. You and I will then tell Inspector Bracket all about the case. I will then officially hand over the keys and resign my position. Then everything is yours,' said Ravenscroft with a note of sadness in his voice.

'What will you do next, sir?'

'Samuel has promised me a holiday in northern France,' said Lucy light-heartedly.

'I am sure that will be very pleasant.'

'After that I do not know,' said Ravenscroft. 'We will have to see what life brings.'

'I cannot quite see you becoming a gardener, sir.'

Ravenscroft laughed. 'Growing vegetables and tending roses have never been my specialities.'

'There is always time to learn,' said Lucy encouragingly.

'Now, Tom, have you had any more thoughts about the case?' asked Ravenscroft, quickly changing the subject.

'Not really, although I am inclined to agree with you that the Moncriefs probably did not kill Adam Pendleton. That leaves Marcus Snaith as the chief suspect,' answered Crabb.

'Surely a man would not kill his own nephew,' said Lucy.

'Some killers have been known to murder even closer relatives than nephews,' said Ravenscroft. 'Did the two of them fall out over their planned deception, so that Snaith killed his nephew to keep him quiet? It is possible, of course.'

'There's still Mr Fanshawe,' said Crabb.

'Yes, we know he was putting pressure on Maud Fincher to sell Claremont to him, so that he could build his luxury hotel in Colwall, and he may have made a similar offer to her cousin, but we have already discounted that, remember. Killing the heir would make it harder to buy Claremont, not easier,' replied Ravenscroft.

'It seems we are going round in circles,' remarked Crabb.

'Well, I have been thinking things over, and I have come to the conclusion that you have both been missing one line of enquiry in all of this,' said Lucy.

'Go on?' asked a curious Ravenscroft.

'You do not know what Maud Fincher's secret was.'

'Explain further.'

'You know that Maud Fincher fell out with her parents all those years ago, and that she then came to live in Colwall.

If you can find out why she left Cirencester that might help you to solve the case. It seems pretty straightforward to me.'

'Do you know, my dear, you could be right,' said Ravenscroft, leaning back in his chair.

'It all seems quite sensible to me,' added Lucy, sounding pleased with herself.

'The Moncriefs did say that Maud Fincher was anxious to obtain her parent's forgiveness,' said Crabb.

'What time is it, Crabb?' asked Ravenscroft.

'Just three minutes past eight o'clock.'

'Where is the Bradshaw?'

'On the desk over there,' replied Lucy.

Ravenscroft sprang up from his chair, walked over to the book and quickly thumbed through the pages, as Crabb and Lucy looked at one another with puzzled expressions on their faces.

'Right, put your coat on, my dear. Susan can look after young Arthur for the day. If we are quick we can catch the eight thirty. Tom, you will have to go and see Bracket yourself.'

'What will I say to him?' asked Crabb.

'Tell him that I have gone fishing, or that I have been called away to attend a sick relative. I will leave it to you to come up with something. Tell him that I will see him as soon as I return, whenever that will be. You can tell him all about the case, but don't say that I have gone to Cirencester. I don't want him following me out there trying to improve his detective skills, when after all we may find nothing.'

'As you wish, sir.'

'Lucy, I should have listened to you earlier. We have been so absorbed in following this case along certain avenues that we may have failed to take the more obvious path. Come, we must make all speed! This could be our last chance.'

* * *

Later that morning Ravenscroft and Lucy alighted from the train at Cirencester Town Station.

'Do you think you could find your way back to the Finchers' house?' asked Ravenscroft.

'I believe so,' replied Lucy.

'I should have listened to you properly when you returned from Cirencester the first time.'

'Other more pressing matters intervened.'

'Like the death of Adam Pendleton. I suppose we were so involved in discovering his identity, and where he came from, that we completely forgot about what you had found out in Cirencester.'

'Well, we are here now, Samuel, and who knows what we will discover,' said Lucy, giving her husband's arm an encouraging squeeze.

The couple walked through the streets of the town until they reached the house Lucy had viewed on her previous visit.

'Apparently that was where Jasper and Margaret Fincher and their daughter Maud Fincher lived, and later where the real Rupert Fincher resided until his untimely death, according to what the old gravedigger Giles Strongbow told me,' said Lucy.

'I see what you meant when you said that the property was in a sorry state,' replied Ravenscroft looking across the road at the uncared-for house. 'Clearly no one has lived here since Rupert Fincher died eight years ago.'

'It is rather sad really. Properties only seem to have a life when there are people to live in them, and once they have gone, it is as if the house slowly dies,' reflected Lucy.

'It would be good if we could get inside. I will try the front door, but expect it is securely locked.' Ravenscroft pushed on the woodwork to see if it would give way. 'No, it is as I thought.'

'What about going round the back?' said Lucy. 'There appears to be a door in the wall at the side of the property that might lead somewhere.'

They went to the door and Ravenscroft tried it. 'This seems quite stiff. But if I give it another push . . . Ah, it gives way. You are right, my dear, it does open up on to a passageway, which I hope will take us round the back.'

The couple walked down the narrow alleyway and into a small yard at the rear of the property.

'That is the back door. Let me try that. No, it is securely locked. My guess is that it is bolted from the inside. How frustrating, to come all this way only to be prevented from gaining access to the house,' said Ravenscroft.

'What about the window,' suggested Lucy.

'I suppose there might be just a chance,' said Ravenscroft. 'There is a very small gap, no bigger than half an inch, at the bottom of the frame. It is too small and narrow for me to get my fingers underneath. What we need is something we can slide in.'

'That old tile should do the trick,' said Lucy, pointing behind them to a pile of debris that lay in the corner of the yard.

'Excellent,' said Ravenscroft. 'If I push half the tile through the gap, and then lean down on the other half, then I might just be able to raise it enough to get my hand underneath and push the frame upwards.'

'Be careful not to trap your fingers, Samuel.'

'Ah, there we are!' exclaimed Ravenscroft. 'Now, if you could hold the frame in place while I climb through . . .'

Ravenscroft inched his body through the gap and disappeared into the dark interior, as Lucy looked on anxiously.

'Damn it!' shouted Ravenscroft from inside the house.

'What is it Samuel?' called Lucy.

'Nothing! I've just trod on a mousetrap. I'll try to open the back door.'

Lucy waited as she heard the slow drawing back of the bolts.

'There we are,' said Ravenscroft opening the door.

'Are you alright?'

'Yes thank you, it was just the sudden shock, but there is no harm done,' said Ravenscroft brushing off some dust from his coat. 'Be careful as you enter, you just don't know what lies waiting in these old houses.'

'As long as it is not old Jasper's remains lying on his bed, or a collection of rats and mice, I think I will be fine.'

'This seems to be the back hallway. Let's make our way into the main rooms. I will go first and see if I can open the shutters to let in more light, so we can find our way around,' said Ravenscroft pushing open the door, which opened out on to a much larger hallway. 'Stay here, while I go in there.'

Ravenscroft opened the door cautiously and in the half-light made his way to the front window, where he opened the shutters so that the room was bathed in morning sunlight.

'All the furniture has been covered over with these old sheets,' said Lucy. 'They are coated in dust, and just look at all those cobwebs in the corners of the ceiling.'

'Sofa, chairs, table — we must be in the main living room or parlour,' said Ravenscroft lifting up each of the sheets and looking underneath.

'What are you looking for?' asked Lucy.

'I won't know until I have found it. If we are to discover what Maud Fincher's secret was then I need to find out as much as I can about the family.'

'What a most unattractive painting that is,' said Lucy, staring up at a large portrait hanging above the fireplace.

'Not a particularly great work of art, I'm inclined to agree with you. It was probably painted in the last century, by some jobbing artist. Perhaps it is some Fincher ancestor,' said Ravenscroft. 'There is a desk underneath this sheet, but unfortunately there are no papers or letters or indeed anything else in the drawers. I'll close the shutters, and we will go and have a look in the other main room.'

A few seconds later Lucy and Ravenscroft found themselves standing in what appeared to be the dining room of the house. Again Ravenscroft opened the shutters, and they then lifted up the sheets to reveal a large table and various chairs.

'I fancy that portrait is the other one of the pair,' said Ravenscroft looking above the mantelpiece. 'It must be the wife of the man in the other room.'

'She certainly wasn't a beauty,' remarked Lucy.

'There is nothing here of a personal nature,' said Ravenscroft, after the search of the room had been made. 'We will see what there is upstairs.'

Ravenscroft and Lucy made their way up the main staircase and found themselves standing on a landing with three doors leading off.

'This seems to be the main bedroom,' remarked Ravenscroft, after he had opened the shutters in one of the rooms. 'Perhaps it was where Rupert Fincher lived until his demise, and Jasper and Margaret Fincher before him. If you could look in the wardrobe, I will go through the drawers.'

'There is nothing here,' said Lucy. 'It is completely bare.'

'The same here. The drawers are completely empty.'

'The executors must have cleared out all his clothes and personal possessions after Rupert Fincher died.'

'It would seem so. Let us go and see if we can find anything in the other rooms.'

Lucy followed her husband into the second bedroom.

'I suppose this was the guest bedroom, or Maud Fincher's bedroom when she was a young girl, but again every drawer is empty,' said Ravenscroft when he had completed his search.

Ravenscroft and Lucy closed the shutters behind them and walked along the corridor towards the third bedroom.

'Door is a bit stiff; I fancy this room was the least used,' said Ravenscroft, pushing hard against the woodwork.

The door slowly edged open, and they stepped into a small airless dusty room, where almost threadbare curtains hung loosely from the windows, and various books littered the floor.

'It must be the old nursery,' said Lucy, going up to the rocking horse in the corner of the room.

'And that is where Maud Fincher must have slept as a child,' added Ravenscroft. 'There are two bedrooms fifty or sixty years apart; the one in Colwall where Maud Fincher died, and this one where she slept and played when she was a child.'

'It is all rather sad, to see it like this, and to know the story behind it.'

'Maud was an only child,' said Ravenscroft, 'and when she grew up this room must have been abandoned. Rupert Fincher must have left it as it was, and there were no further generations of Fincher children to occupy it. As you say, my dear, it is sad to see it like this, unloved and neglected.'

'It is so cold in here,' said Lucy, shivering.

'Yes, I think we should leave. I can find nothing of a personal nature here that might lead us onwards in our search for Maud Fincher's secret. If only Rupert Fincher had not died eight years ago, we might have been able to learn something from him.' Ravenscroft gave a resigned sigh. 'I am sorry to have dragged you all the way out here again, on what has proved to be a forlorn quest.'

'What is that in the other corner of the room?' said Lucy.

Ravenscroft crossed over and reached down. 'It appears to be pieces of a card of some sort. I wonder if it is of some importance. I cannot read what it says but if we collect all the pieces and lay them on the bed, we may be able to join them up. Someone must have discarded the pieces on the floor all those years ago.'

'It is like a jigsaw puzzle,' remarked Lucy as her husband moved the eight or ten pieces around on the bed until they formed a whole.

'There is some printing on it. "Snittering and Son, Solicitors, Coxwell Street, Cirencester." It's a business card. I wonder if this Snittering was the Fincher family solicitor.'

'There is only one way to find out,' said Lucy.

'You are right. We will pay a visit to Snittering and Son. But first, let us try to leave the house as we found it, then I will bolt the door and climb out of the back window.'

'And what about me?' asked Lucy.

'Oh you can leave by the back door, unless, of course, you prefer to step over the mousetraps to exit through the window,' said Ravenscroft light-heartedly.

* * *

Ravenscroft and Lucy made their way back to the market-place in the centre of Cirencester, where the ancient parish church stood tall and imposing.

'Good morning, I wonder if you could direct us to Coxwell Street,' said Ravenscroft, addressing a man who was standing outside the entrance to the church smoking an old wooden pipe.

'Why it is Mr Strongbow, is it not?' said Lucy, recognising the man whom she had seen on her previous visit to the town.

'Good morning to ye,' replied the man, after removing his pipe from his mouth.

'Samuel, this is Mr Strongbow, who was of great value to me,' said Lucy.

'Then I am indebted to you, sir,' said Ravenscroft.

'Glad to have been of assistance,' said Giles Strongbow. 'If ye goes down that road there, and take first left, that be Coxwell Street

'Thank you. We are looking for the offices of Mr Snittering.'

'That means trouble.'

'Oh, why do you say that?'

'People only goes to those kind of places when they thinks they is going to die. My great aunt went to see Snittering, and three days later she was dead,' muttered Strongbow, before resuming his smoking.

'That must have just been a coincidence, surely,' said Ravenscroft.

'You tells me, you looks like a policeman to me.'

'That is very observant of you,' said Ravenscroft smiling. 'When did this great aunt of yours die?'

'It were forty-three years ago this Tuesday.'

'Rather a long time ago.'

'They said she died of the flux but I knows different. She caught something nasty from old man Snittering. She was fine when she went into his office, dead three days later.

Course, if she had put a frog in her mouth she might have been alright.'

'A frog?' asked Lucy.

'Yes, they says round these parts that if you holds a frog to the mouth of a sick one, and the person who is ill breathes into the mouth of the frog, you will be cured,' replied Strongbow, gesturing wildly and clearly enjoying his subject.

'It sounds perfectly horrible to me,' exclaimed Lucy.

'Why didn't your aunt follow this advice?' asked Ravenscroft, before almost wishing that he had not asked the question.

'She couldn't find any frogs,' replied Strongbow.

'I am sorry to hear it. I can see we will have to take care. If you could direct us to Snittering and Son, we would be most obliged,' said Ravenscroft, amused.

'Third building on the left as you goes down Coxwell Street.'

'Thank you, Mr Strongbow.'

'You minds how you goes,' sniggered Strongbow.

'We will,' said Ravenscroft as he and Lucy walked away. 'What a strange man your Mr Strongbow is.'

'That frog story sounds highly unlikely.'

'Oh, I wouldn't say that. There are many ancient superstitions that are still prevalent in these parts of the country.'

A few minutes later, Ravenscroft and Lucy came to a half-timbered building in Coxwell Street. A creaking sign with faded lettering proclaimed they had reached the offices of Snittering and Sons.

Ravenscroft pushed open the door, and he and Lucy walked up the old wooden stairs, which bought them to a door at top of the flight. The detective opened the door cautiously.

'Ah, good morning to you both,' said a small wrinkled man with greying hair and a red nose, who came forward to meet them.

Ravenscroft removed his hat. 'Do I have the honour of addressing Mr Snittering?'

'You do indeed. Please take a seat, and your good lady as well,' said the solicitor wiping down two wooden chairs with a large cloth and coughing loudly as he did so.

'Thank you,' said Ravenscroft as he and Lucy sat down.

'Now then, how may I be of assistance? A will to be drawn up, transfer of assets, a house purchase perhaps?' said Snittering, coughing again as he seated himself behind the partners desk.

'No, nothing like that,' said Ravenscroft.

'That is a pity. There are many fine properties in the town which are for sale at present, and which might suit such a gentleman as yourself and your fine lady,' *cough, cough.*

'No, sir. My name is Detective Inspector Ravenscroft, and I require some information regarding the Fincher family. I believe you may have acted for the family in the past.'

'That is correct. I was involved with the estate of Mr Rupert Fincher, and I believe that my late father, Mr Jabez Snittering, the founder of the firm, may have been involved with the affairs of earlier family members,' *cough, cough.* 'But may I ask how you have learned of our involvement in this matter?'

'We found a business card with your name on it inside Rupert Fincher's house,' said Ravenscroft.

'Really? May I ask how you came by such a business card?' asked Snittering, giving Ravenscroft a suspicious look out of the corner of his eye.

'I must confess, Mr Snittering, that I was able to enter the house through a back window.'

'Good Lord! That is highly irregular.'

'Indeed, but I am a police officer investigating a most serious matter, and the window was open, and everything has been left as we found it, so I do not think that any offence has been committed.'

'I see. Well this is still rather irregular,' said Snittering looking over the top of his spectacles at the detective and coughing as he did so. 'You say that you are investigating a serious matter?'

'Yes. It would be of great value to us if you could let me see any documents you may have in your possession regarding the Fincher family.'

'Well, yes, I suppose I could do that.'

The solicitor stood up, cleaned his spectacles vigorously on a large brown handkerchief, coughed, and then walked over to one of the many piles of folders that littered the floor of the room.

'Now let me see. Fincher, Fincher . . . If you could just hold these files for me.' Snittering lifted up the top half of one of the piles and passed the contents to Ravenscroft. 'Now if you would do the same, my good lady,' he continued, passing yet more files to Lucy. 'Ah, here we are: Fincher. That which has been sadly neglected all these long years has been carried forth into the sunlight once more. Now if I take those files from you, I will return them to their correct positions in the pile. Yes, that is most satisfactory, most satisfactory indeed.' *Cough, cough.*

Ravenscroft and Lucy resumed their seats as Snittering sat down and blew off the dust that had accumulated on the outside of the folder.

'Now let me see — ah, yes, it appears that we have the will and last testament of one Jasper Fincher of Cirencester,' said Snittering, studying the contents of the folder. 'I see it was drawn up by my late father, Jabez, and is dated 10 April 1847.'

'What does the will say?' asked Ravenscroft eagerly.

'Yes, yes, ah here we are — "I leave all my possessions to my beloved dutiful daughter, Maud Fincher, to be given to her upon my death."'

'Forgive me Mr Snittering, but if the estate was left to Maud Fincher, how was it that Rupert Fincher inherited everything?'

'Ah, yes, a very good question indeed.' *Cough, cough.* 'Ah, I see there is a codicil to the will, dated 7 May 1861. Oh dear me, this might explain everything.'

'Yes, do please go on,' said Ravenscroft leaning forward in his chair.

'Yes, well here we are. "To my daughter, Maud Fincher, I leave nothing, except the annuity which will be made for her, because of her indiscreet and foolish behaviour. My estate will pass upon my death to any surviving children of my younger brother, Francis Fincher and his wife." Well, well, that is an interesting state of affairs indeed.' *Cough, cough.*

'Maud Fincher's indiscreet and foolish behaviour — what does that mean?' asked Lucy.

'It means that Jasper Fincher disinherited his daughter,' said Ravenscroft. 'In 1847 she was his "beloved, dutiful daughter," and fourteen years later she had disgraced the family in some way.'

Snittering retrieved his handkerchief from his pocket and coughed loudly into it for several seconds.

'Can I get you something for that cough, Mr Snittering?' asked Lucy.

'That is most kind of you, my good lady, but there is no need, I assure you. I have had this cough for many long years, boy and man, and when I die, which I expect to do quite shortly, my cough will no doubt live on after me.'

'I am sorry to hear that. They do say a frog can cure a bad cough,' said Lucy.

'A frog?' asked the bewildered solicitor.

Ravenscroft quickly changed the subject. 'So that is how Rupert Fincher came to inherit the property. You say, Mr Snittering, that you dealt with the estate when Mr Rupert Fincher inherited it?'

'Yes, that is correct. When Jasper Fincher died some twelve years ago, I contacted Rupert Fincher, the sole child of Jasper's younger brother, and informed him of his inheritance. He then moved into the old family property, but alas was carried away with the dreadful scarlet fever four years later.' *Cough, cough.*

'I assume that Mr Rupert Fincher had no wife or issue?' asked Ravenscroft.

'That is correct. Since Mr Fincher's demise, the house has been locked up and the assets frozen, as it were, until at such time as another claimant comes forward.'

'That would seem unlikely. Mr Snittering, are there any other documents in the file? It would be of value to us to learn what indiscretion had been committed by Maud Fincher that resulted in her disinheritance.'

'Let me see. Ah, yes, there is indeed another document,' coughed Snittering, bringing out another piece of paper from the folder. 'It would seem to be an agreement of some sort made between Jasper Fincher and his daughter, Maud Fincher, dated 7 May 7 1861.'

'The same date as the codicil attached to the will,' said Lucy.

'I wonder if I might examine the document?' asked Ravenscroft.

The solicitor passed over the paper to Ravenscroft, who then read out the contents.

> 'This agreement is signed on the 7 May 1861, between Jasper Fincher of Cirencester and his daughter, Maud Fincher. I, Jasper Fincher, give unto my daughter, Maud Fincher, the payment of one hundred pounds, and the interest on an annuity which is placed at Barings Bank in London, to be paid to her during her lifetime, on the following two conditions: 1. That the said Maud Fincher is to leave Cirencester for ever and that she is never to return and see her parents again, on forfeiture of the said annuity. 2. That the said Maud Fincher gives up her bastard child to a suitable institution for adoption, and that she is never to see the said child ever again during her lifetime.'

'How absolutely terrible!' exclaimed Lucy. 'The poor woman, forced to give up her only child like that.'

'The terms do seem rather harsh, I must admit, but of course Jasper Fincher was fully entitled to make such terms, as indeed was Maud Fincher to accept them,' said Snittering.

'She signed the document?' enquired Lucy.

'Yes, indeed, there is her signature,' indicated Ravenscroft.

'She gave up her child for the sake of a hundred pounds and an annual annuity,' said Lucy. 'What mother would do such a thing?'

'She probably had little choice — keeping the child would likely mean penury for both of them. Instead, she purchased the house in Colwall, where she remained for the rest of her life, and lived on this annuity. It also explains why she never returned to Cirencester. To have done so would have resulted in the annulment of the annuity,' said Ravenscroft.

'Forgive me, but you speak of Miss Fincher in the past tense. Am I to assume that the good lady is deceased?' *Cough, cough.*

'She is indeed, and a young man impersonating Rupert Fincher has been killed in a cruel way,' said Ravenscroft firmly.

'Good heavens! This means that I will have to write to Barings directly and inform them of the good lady's demise.'

'Well thank you, Mr Snittering, you have been of great assistance to us,' said Ravenscroft, standing up and pushing back his chair.

'I am glad that I have been able to help you,' smiled Snittering, before coughing loudly into his handkerchief once more.

'Oh, just one more question, Mr Snittering, if you will. The agreement speaks of Maud Fincher having to give up her child to a suitable institution for adoption. That would suggest an orphanage. Where was the nearest orphanage to Cirencester in those days?' asked Ravenscroft.

'That would most likely be in Cheltenham.'

'Thank you, Mr Snittering. We wish you good day.'

Ravenscroft and Lucy quickly left the room and made their way down the steps and out into the street, the sound of coughing decreasing in volume as they did so.

* * *

'I cannot but feel sorry for the poor woman,' said Lucy as their cab made its way along the streets of Cheltenham. 'She was compelled to abandon her only child like that. Her father seems such an unfeeling man.'

'He did not want the disgrace to fall upon his family and situation. Cirencester is a small provincial town where everyone knows everyone else. He could not afford the scandal,' said Ravenscroft.

'She could have kept the baby.'

'But then she would have become destitute, cut off from her family and without a penny to her name, her baby would probably have died through want. Taking the annuity and the money to buy the house in Colwall was her only way out of her predicament.'

'But at a terrible cost.'

'I suppose that was why Maud Fincher was on the local fundraising committee for Doctor Barnardo's Homes. That was her atonement. She had given away her own child, and she saw that as a way of coming to terms with her own guilt. I should have realised that from the start when the Chief Constable told me that both his wife and Maud Fincher were on the same committee.'

'You were not to know that at the time.'

'Poor Maud Fincher had to live with what she had done for the rest of her life, and then when the Moncriefs arrived in Malvern it must have seemed that the past had been created anew.'

'The Moncriefs used Silas Crabbit to play upon the poor woman's mind, driving her to an early grave.'

'Tell me, Lucy, was there ever a time when Richard was born that you considered the possibility of giving him up?' asked Ravenscroft.

'When I was waiting for him to be born, I was resolved to do so, but after his birth I knew in my heart that I could never abandon him. Then I came to Ledbury and later met you, so everything has worked out for the best,' replied Lucy, gently squeezing her husband's arm.

'And I treasure the day that happened,' smiled Ravenscroft.

'Do you think that the answer to all this involves the lost child of Maud Fincher?'

'I do not know, but now that we have uncovered her dark secret, we must follow the trail further and see where it takes us. Of course, there is no guarantee that we will be successful. Maud Fincher may have taken her child to an orphanage that we cannot discover, or the child may have died in infancy. Either so, I am determined to see this through.'

'What if this child later sought out its mother?'

'That is an interesting speculation—''Orphanage, governor!' shouted out the cabman, pulling the horse to a standstill.

'Here you are, my man,' said Ravenscroft handing the cabman a coin, before helping Lucy to alight. 'Do you think you could wait for us? We will probably need to go to the railway station after our visit.'

'That all depends on how long you is going to be,' replied the cabman.

'Shall we say thirty minutes at the most,' replied Ravenscroft, handing the cabman another coin.

'Thank you, sir. God bless you. I reckons the horse could do with a rest anyway.'

Ravenscroft and Lucy looked up at the austere grey-stone building, before walking up to the large oak front door and ringing the bell.

A middle-aged woman dressed in nursing attire greeted them at the door.

'Good afternoon. My name is Detective Inspector Ravenscroft and this is my wife. I wonder if we might take a few minutes of your time.'

The woman looked seriously through her wire framed spectacles at the detective.

'We need some information concerning one of your former charges,' continued Ravenscroft.

'You had best follow me, then,' replied the woman opening the door wider.

Ravenscroft and Lucy entered, and followed the woman down a long drab corridor until they reached an office at the end. Nearby they could hear the sound of a child crying, and the strong smell of carbolic soap hung in the air.

The woman indicated that Lucy and Ravenscroft were to take seats before a small desk. 'My name is Mrs Ethel Jacob. I am the matron of the orphanage.'

'I will come straight to the point, Mrs Jacob. We require information regarding a child that may have been given to your orphanage in May 1861,' said Ravenscroft.

'I am afraid that I cannot help you. I was not here then, and anyway it is against our rules to give out any confidential information regarding destitute children who are admitted here,' said Mrs Jacob, in a voice that seemed to Ravenscroft to be both clinical and detached.

'I am at present investigating the murders of two people, and one of the chief suspects may be the very person that we require information about,' countered Ravenscroft.

'As I have just said, Inspector, information regarding our orphans is strictly confidential, and is not to be disclosed to anyone.'

'The child would have entered this establishment in 1861. That was thirty-two years ago. As that child has long since grown to maturity and has since left the orphanage, then I do not see the difficulty. Two people have been murdered. If I am to bring the perpetrator to justice — and prevent anyone else from losing their lives in this way — then it is imperative that you assist us in our enquiries. I can also assure you that what we learn in this room will remain just between ourselves, Mrs Jacob,' said Ravenscroft trying to sound as serious as he could.

Mrs Jacob looked intently at Ravenscroft, and then at Lucy, without saying a word, before crossing over to a large bookcase at the side of the room. 'You said May 1861?'

She picked out one of the large volumes from the shelf and returned to her seat behind the desk. Ravenscroft and

Lucy glanced at each other with anxious expressions on their faces, as the woman turned over the pages in the volume.

'Yes, here we are. On 9 May 1861: an infant child found on the steps of the orphanage, and taken into care,' said Mrs Jacob, reading from the page.

'Just two days after the agreement and the codicil,' said Lucy.

'There is no information regarding the child's mother?' asked Ravenscroft.

'No, it would appear not.'

'Do you have many babies who are abandoned in this way?' asked Lucy.

'Some mothers who have fallen on hard times, or who have been disgraced, seek out the orphanage to take care of their babies.'

'Do any of these parents ever return?' continued Lucy.

'It is quite rare for a mother to do so.'

'Were there any other entries for abandoned infants from around the same period?' asked Ravenscroft.

'No, the only similar entry, of a child being abandoned, is not until two years later,' said Mrs Jacob, after studying the following two pages.

'I see. As this child was abandoned here, how did you record the child's future progress?' enquired Ravenscroft.

'The child was allocated a number — 1015, in this case.'

'Does the entry record any other details?'

'Yes, apparently a small silver locket was left with the child.'

'That is interesting. And this was a common practice?'

'Oh yes, it was one way, perhaps the only way, in which a mother might reclaim her child should she return later to the orphanage. Any such tokens would be placed in the child's docket.'

'And if the mother did not return?' asked Lucy.

'Then, when it was time for the child to leave the orphanage the token, or keepsake, would be given to the child.'

'Can you tell us any more about this child, Mrs Jacob?' said Ravenscroft.

'This was before my time, as I have said. I have only been matron here for the past ten years, but there is a date recorded next to the entry, which refers to a later event,' said Mrs Jacob.

'Could we see what the later entry is?' asked the detective eagerly.

Mrs Jacob rose from her seat, and crossed over to the shelves in silence, where she replaced the first volume and selected another one.

'Yes, here we are,' she said after a minute or so had passed in the silent room. 'In 1869 the child was allocated to a couple living near Stroud.'

'What do you mean by "allocated"?' asked Ravenscroft.

'When our orphaned children are considered old enough they may be apprenticed, or put into service,' explained Mrs Jacob. 'Sometimes the child may be formally adopted. This is what appears to have happened on this occasion. After that, there are no further entries.'

'But the child was only eight years old!' exclaimed Lucy.

'It is quite common practice that if a suitable person requests such a child, and after enquiries have been made as to their suitability, permission is then often granted.'

'That seems to be quite harsh, at such a tender age,' protested Lucy.

'We are not a charity here Mrs Ravenscroft. We cannot afford to look after these abandoned children indefinitely. Such a child can prove to be a drain on our financial resources. It is far better if a suitable opportunity presents itself that we should embrace such an offer on the child's behalf. Boys can be apprenticed to a tradesman or work on the farms, whereas the girls can enter service. Thereby the orphan has an opportunity later to become a useful member of society.'

'Can you give us the name of the family near Stroud that the child was adopted by?' asked Ravenscroft.

'I am not sure I can do that.'

'It is imperative that you do so. We must know what happened to the child,' stressed Ravenscroft, leaning forward in his seat.

Mrs Jacob gave the detective a cold look for some seconds, before reluctantly pushing the ledger across the table in the detective's direction.

'Thank you, Mrs Jacob. Good heavens!' exclaimed Ravenscroft. 'Look here, Lucy, do you see that name? That explains everything. Up until now, I assumed that this child was a boy.'

'Oh that is not the case — the child was not a boy. Number 1015 was a girl!'

CHAPTER SIXTEEN

Dusk was beginning to fall as Ravenscroft, Crabb and Bracket knocked loudly on the old oak door.

'Inspector Ravenscroft!' said Gladys Brotherton, opening the door of Claremont.

'Good evening, Gladys. I would be obliged if we could enter and ask you a few questions,' said Ravenscroft. 'Sergeant Crabb you have met before. This other gentleman is Inspector Bracket.'

'Yes, yes, you had better enter,' said the maid, visibly taken aback by the sudden arrival of the three men.

'I see you are leaving, Gladys,' said Ravenscroft, noticing the two cases in the hallway.

'Yes, I have today informed Mr Snaith that I can do no more here. I think it best if I seek employment elsewhere. There is nothing else for me in this place. I will shortly be taking the evening train to London.'

'Then it is fortunate that we have caught you,' said Ravenscroft.

'You had best come into the drawing room,' said the maid, leading the way.

'Now, Gladys, we have been making further investigations regarding your late mistress, Miss Maud Fincher,' said

Ravenscroft when the party had seated themselves. 'When did you realise that Miss Fincher was your mother?'

A moment's silence elapsed before Gladys protested, 'I am sorry, I don't know what you are talking about.'

'Today I visited the orphanage in Cheltenham, where I discovered that in May 1861, an infant child was abandoned on the steps of the institution. The mother of that child was Maud Fincher. The child spent the first eight years of its life in the orphanage, before being adopted by a couple near Stroud, by the name of Brotherton. I have reason to believe that you were that child. Am I not correct?'

The maid said nothing as tears began to form in her eyes.

'When Maud Fincher left the child at the orphanage, she left a token, a keepsake, a locket. I observe that you are wearing such a locket round your neck.'

Again the maid said nothing as she covered her face with her hands.

'When did you first know that Maud Fincher was your mother?' continued Ravenscroft.

Gladys Brotherton emitted a loud sob from beneath her hands.

'Can I get you some water?' asked Bracket.

'No, thank you. You are correct, Inspector, Maud Fincher was indeed my natural mother,' said Gladys Brotherton through her tears. 'I did not know that until the night she died.'

'Could you elaborate further?' urged Ravenscroft.

'Do you know what it was like living in that orphanage? Knowing that my mother had abandoned me shortly after my birth? How could she have done that? The other children ignored me. I was so unhappy and lonely. It was as though I had no right to even exist. Then one day they said a couple wanted to raise me as their own, and I thought that at long last I would be able to escape from the orphanage and lead a better life, but it was not to be. They gave me their name and that was all. I thought that this couple had chosen me for who I was, and that they would care for me, but I soon found out that all they wanted was someone to clean and wash and wait upon them. They both treated me harshly. I would lie in bed at night, crying and praying that one day my real mother would come and reclaim me.

'As I grew older, I found myself longing for the day when I could leave and make my own way in the world. Then when I was fifteen, I left. I went to London and gained employment in various establishments during the following years. There was a young man who said he wanted to marry me, but I could not bring myself to accept him. I feared that there would be a child, and that my lover would abandon me, and that I would be forced to give the child away, as my mother had done. I did not want that. Then one day, about seven months ago, my master and mistress went abroad. I looked for another position. That is how I came here to Claremont.'

'You saw the advertisement for a maid in one of the national newspapers?' asked Ravenscroft.

'Yes.'

'And you had no idea that Miss Fincher was your mother until the night she died?' Ravenscroft's tone was sympathetic. 'Can you tell us what happened that night?'

'My mistress woke in the middle of the night. She called out that she felt unwell. I went into the bedroom. I was wearing this locket round my neck. I had never worn it before in her presence; it was only at night when I was alone in my room alone that I would sometime put it around my neck and wonder who its owner had been. My mistress saw the locket, and she knew then that I was her daughter.' Gladys Brotherton wiped the tears away from her eyes.

'That must have been distressing for both of you,' said Ravenscroft. 'Can you tell us what happened next?'

'The shock was too great for her. She collapsed on the floor. I knew she was dead.'

Ravenscroft said nothing for a few moments, as he considered deeply how best to proceed.

'I think you and your mother argued,' suggested Bracket, interrupting Ravenscroft's thoughts.

'No, no, there was no argument. We were reunited for that brief second, then it was all taken away,' cried Gladys Brotherton. 'All those years I had waited. It was cruel.'

'So what did you do next?' asked Ravenscroft, adopting a more assertive tone.

'I could do nothing. I just sat there looking down at her, wishing that she would come alive. Then when dawn arrived I went and fetched Doctor Cranbrook.'

'Shall I tell you what I think really happened?' said Ravenscroft.

Gladys Brotherton said nothing as she cried into her hands.

'You grew up resenting your mother for giving you up, and all the suffering you had endured as a child and as a woman. While she had been living in quiet comfortable seclusion in Colwall, you had been forced to earn your living serving others. I think you learned that Miss Fincher was your natural mother shortly after you came here, and that you grew to hate her even more for what she had done to you all those years ago, but instead of telling her that you were her daughter, you decided to take revenge.'

'No, no, this is not true,' sobbed Gladys Brotherton.

'Then one day the Moncriefs arrived in Malvern, and your mother attended their séances. Here she encountered Silas Crabbit, who claimed through Janet Moncrief, that she could speak with her dead parents. But you and I both know that this was all nonsense. Nevertheless you played on all of this all of this, causing your mistress great distress as she encountered the past again, so much so that she eventually began to fear for her life. I think you finally confronted your mother that night, a violent argument ensued — and that you caused her death.'

'I have told you the truth. You will never be able to prove otherwise,' retorted Gladys Brotherton, adopting a more defensive manner.

'You may well be right. That will be for a jury to decide. Why did you kill Adam Pendleton, or rather, the man you thought was Rupert Fincher?'

'I did not kill him.'

'I think you were hoping that one day when all this had died down, you would return and claim your rightful inheritance as Maud Fincher's daughter. You had not considered the possibility that another claimant would come forward first and deprive you of that legacy,' said Ravenscroft firmly, realising that he was finally about to solve the case.

'And why should that spoilt brat have what was rightfully mine?' snapped Gladys Brotherton, her cheeks becoming suddenly red with anger. 'All these years I have toiled and worked for others. My life has been a misery, all because she abandoned me all those years ago? Surely I deserve some kind of justice for all that I have endured? Then at last I had the chance to make something of my life, but that arrogant pompous man came to the funeral saying he was Maud's cousin and that everything was his.'

'So you lured him to the Priory Gardens?' continued Ravenscroft.

'Yes, but I only wanted to tell him that I was Maud Fincher's daughter, that it was I and not him that was entitled to inherit her estate, but he just laughed at me, saying I was just a simple servant who should know her place, and that I should leave the area as soon as possible or he would set the law on me.'

'So in a fit of anger you picked up a stones and struck the fatal blow?' prompted Ravenscroft.

'He turned away from me, laughing. I could not stand him mocking me like that,' said Gladys Brotherton.

Ravenscroft remained silent for a moment, looking down at the floor, before turning to Bracket. 'Inspector, you must do your duty.'

'Gladys Brotherton, you are to be taken into custody on suspicion of causing the deaths of Maud Fincher and Adam

Pendleton. You should be careful what you say, as it may be given in evidence against you. Come with us now.'

* * *

Later that evening, the three detectives stood in the outer room of Ledbury Police Station.

'Well that is done. Gladys Brotherton is safely on her way to Worcester Jail,' said Bracket. Do you think she really killed her mother?'

'I don't know. Gladys Brotherton might have been telling us the truth. Perhaps the shock of discovering that her maid was her long-lost daughter may indeed have caused Maud Fincher to die, or the pair might have argued and Gladys caused her mother's death. There was a great deal of hate and resentment there.'

'We may never know the whole story of what happened in that bedroom that night,' said Bracket.

'Do you know what is most ironic about this case?' said Ravenscroft. 'Gladys Brotherton thought she had killed Rupert Fincher in the Priory Gardens, believing that she could later return and claim the estate. What she did not know was that the man was an imposter. Rupert Fincher was already dead. All she had to do was to expose Adam Pendleton as an imposter, and she would then have been able to claim the inheritance. She did not need to kill him at all.'

'So it was all for nothing?' asked Bracket.

'It would appear so, although when Pendleton mocked Gladys by the Swan Pool, a lifetime's worth of bitterness and emotion flared up in a moment of sudden anger. She would probably have killed him just for that.'

'I am sure she will hang for both crimes. I cannot thank you enough for drawing the case to its successful conclusion,' added Bracket.

'I am glad that I was able to do so. I do not like leaving things unfinished. I have to thank Mrs Ravenscroft for finally guiding me in the right direction,' said Ravenscroft.

'All the same, it was jolly well done, Ravenscroft.'

'And now it is time that I relinquished my position, and formally hand over everything to you, Bracket. You know where I am should you need any assistance, but I am sure that the two of you will manage things without me,' said Ravenscroft, picking up his hat from the counter.

'May I say it has been a pleasure working with you, sir, for all these years,' said Crabb rather sheepishly.

'I could not have wished for a better sergeant and friend. Now all that remains is for me to say good night. Good night, gentlemen.'

'I hope you enjoy your retirement,' said Bracket, but Ravenscroft said nothing as he opened the door and walked out into the street.

Placing his hat on his head, he began to walk briskly away from the station.

'I thought I would come and bring you home,' said Lucy, coming forwards to meet her husband.

'That is most kind of you, my dear,' said Ravenscroft, linking his arm with that of his wife.

'You must be exhausted.'

'A little tired, yes, but then I have the rest of my retirement to make a recovery.'

A sudden sound caused Ravenscroft to turn and look backwards, where he saw Crabb and Bracket, illuminated in the station window, laughing out loud.

'They seem to be getting on quite well,' said Lucy.

'Yes. I am sure that they will work together quite well. But all that is behind us now. Tomorrow we will send a telegram to the Hotel Gandolphi in Dinard and secure a booking. It will be good to return once more to the place we visited after our marriage,' said Ravenscroft, smiling as the pair walked down the narrow lane.

'Samuel, I have something to tell you,' said Lucy, suddenly stopping.

'What is that, my dear?'

Lucy said nothing but drew her husband's hand closer towards her.

'You are with child?' asked Ravenscroft, excited.

'Yes, Samuel, you are about to become a father again — and I know that this time it will be a girl. We will have a daughter. I would like to call her Anne,' said Lucy, looking into her husband's eyes. 'Anne Ravenscroft.'

'Anne Ravenscroft,' repeated the detective. 'Yes, that would be wonderful. Anne Ravenscroft.'

EPILOGUE

Gladys Brotherton stood trial at the Worcester Assizes for the murders of Maud Fincher and Adam Pendleton. The jury acquitted her of the murder of Maud Fincher — but found her guilty of the murder of Adam Pendleton. She was hanged three months later.

Marcus Snaith retired from his legal practice, but ensured that the wife and children of his nephew, Adam Pendleton, were adequately provided for.

Master John Pendleton joined the Bournville Cricket Club when he came of age and went on to play for England. He always remembered his father.

Claremont was sold but remained in private ownership. Mr Fanshawe was later able to build a hotel in Colwall, which attracted many visitors to the area.

Sergeant Crabb ensured that the Moncriefs returned Mrs Shrewsbury's donation.

Felix and Janet Moncrief left Malvern shortly after the events described in these pages. The local newspaper in Tunbridge Wells announced the arrival of spiritualists in the town.

Ravenscroft and Lucy left for their holiday in Dinard.

The bones of Silas Crabbit still lie entombed in the great cave at Boreley Woods.

THE END

ALSO BY KERRY TOMBS

INSPECTOR RAVENSCROFT DETECTIVE MYSTERIES

Book 1: THE MALVERN MURDERS
Book 2: THE WORCESTER WHISPERERS
Book 3: THE LEDBURY LAMPLIGHTERS
Book 4: THE TEWKESBURY TOMB
Book 5: THE DROITWICH DECEIVERS
Book 6: THE PERSHORE POISONERS
Book 7: THE UPTON UNDERTAKERS
Book 8: THE HEREFORDSHIRE HANGMEN
Book 9: THE BROMSGROVE BOOKSELLER
Book 10: RAVENSCROFT'S LAST CASE

Printed in Great Britain
by Amazon

81443318R00130